Beach Shorts

Royston Ellis & Ruth Smith

Beach Shorts
A collection of short stories for holiday reading

Olympia Publishers
London

www.olympiapublishers.com

OLYMPIA PAPERBACK EDITION

A CIP catalogue record for this title is
available from the British Library.

ISBN: 978-1-80074-095-2

First Published in 2021

Olympia Publishers
Tallis House
2 Tallis Street
London
EC4Y 0AB

Printed in Great Britain

Contents

1. Lord of the Waves

The Windsurf Champion of the World was not happy. Kylo Ganoo stood at the window of his hotel room and looked down from the hotel's fifteenth floor to the ocean, where waves were rolling in and cresting before splashing onto the beach. They were not windsurfing waves but nevertheless he longed to be down on the beach, feeling the sea's spray on his face, instead of being alone in the chilly air-conditioned room with the television. He punched his right fist into the palm of his left hand in exasperation.

He was naked. His muscular torso was honed by years of windsurfing into a beautiful, lean, virile body that was the envy of other windsurfers, and acted like a magnet for women when they saw him in his Speedos on his board, conquering the ocean's fury. He was the world's champion, not just in windsurfing but in his aura of sheer masculinity. He had cultivated a gentle, humble personality that endeared him to windsurfing event organisers (and their wives and daughters) and resulted in him travelling the world displaying his prowess on the oceans.

His physique was perfect, he knew that, and he relished the worship, the fame—and the fun—his body and talent brought him. But as he stared down at the distant beach and sea, knowing he was at the peak of his profession as an international windsurfer, Kylo was haunted by doubt.

He turned away from the window and caught sight of his

reflection in the mirror. He was tall, trim, with a massive chest, arms bulging with muscle and strong thighs, moulded by years of practice, allowing him to manoeuvre deftly in the ocean's currents. His body was bronzed, except for a paler V where his skin was shielded from the sun by his Speedos.

He sighed, reached for his clean briefs from the drawer by the mirror, slipped on a T-shirt with a wind surfer design and the boastful but simple slogan: Kylo, World Champion. He pulled on his brand-name jeans, donated to him by the manufacturer, and spent a few minutes brushing his long locks of dark hair, slightly bleached by the sun, which he decided to let frame his face that evening instead of tying into a ponytail.

He flexed his arm muscles as he gazed at his reflection and was pleased to see how his chest rippled. But he sighed and shook his head sadly. This was the creature he had become, the classic image of a world champion. Handsome, charming, modest, polite for his adoring public, but deep within he knew that wasn't the real Kylo.

He turned away and walked to the door to go down for the awards presentation ceremony. He paused and checked the time on his smart phone. He wanted to be about ten minutes late, to make an entrance when the crowd was there and the ceremony had started.

Then he saw the date. It was a year since the day his childhood sweetheart, Mia, had said she couldn't marry him, a man who spends his days windsurfing and his nights she didn't know where. She had given him an ultimatum, telling him, 'I'm not sharing you with the sea. It will take you one day. I'll give you a year to decide, either the sea or me.'

Kylo wondered if Mia remembered the date, maybe had ringed it in red on her calendar. *Perhaps*, he mused, *she has been counting the days and hours to speak after the year had passed.* But, he realised with a shock, they hadn't actually decided about who would make that call, he or Mia.

He was sure that she would have followed his championships, reading about him in magazines or watching him on television, seeing his victories, the photographs as he held trophies aloft. *Probably,* he thought ruefully, *she would have seen candid pictures of himself with a beautiful woman draped over him, or sitting in the back of a taxi with some full-bosomed chick after leaving a night club.*

The elevator arrived, and he punched the button to take him to the first floor where the awards ceremony was being held, in the hotel's huge auditorium. He was the only person in the elevator, and he gazed at the reflection of his face in the small mirror on its back wall. He grinned at himself.

Ah yes, he could still pass for an eighteen-year-old. Just. In low light. A frown creased his brow and he studied his image more closely. There were a few lines around his eyes that he hadn't noticed before, and deeper ones either side of his mouth. Kylo was horrified. He always used the most expensive sun factor on his skin, and a very special moisturiser.

The lift gently bumped to a halt, and he flicked back his hair, smoothed his jeans, and prepared himself for his entrance. He could, of course, have joined the three hundred guests for the five-course dinner, but he had grown bored with that side of things, the eating and drinking and small talk and 'come-to-bed' glances from the women of all ages (and from some of the men) around the tables. He could have worn a tuxedo or white dinner jacket and bow-tie, like the morons who were already very drunk and braying with false laughter at the comedian on stage who was regaling them with filthy jokes. But Kylo knew what his adoring fans wanted, and this was the reason he wore his famous 'uniform' to ceremonies and ostentatious gatherings—jeans, wind-surfing T-shirt and his sun-streaked dark hair free and flying over his shoulders.

He stood against the back wall of the auditorium, flanked by wine waiters who were watching for the signal of beckoning finger from punters who required a re-fill. He had chosen this particular spot to wait, for the simple reason that there was a long, clear pathway from where he stood to the stage, and where the final trophy stood on the presentation table. When he went to collect it, he would have no obstacles of tables, or people reaching out to touch him or slap him on the back. Once upon a time he had wallowed in this adulation, but of late he had tired of the rather sordid pretension of the whole thing.

The blue comedian had run out of steam, or jokes, and had taken himself off stage, to be replaced by the Master of Ceremonies who would perform the presentation. He was a person Kylo detested and dreaded. A second-rate chat show host who delighted in embarrassing and belittling those who had the misfortune to appear as his favoured guests. Only last year, when Kylo had been handed the massive cup for becoming World Champion Windsurfer, the ghastly little man had joked, into the microphone for all to hear 'And still Kylo turns up, year after year! Don't you think he should give someone else a chance?' Laughing at his own joke, the bastard pretended to drop the trophy.

The compere picked the award up and, pretending to sag under its weight, announced, "And the winner of this year's Sport's Personality of the Universe is ..." He paused for dramatic effect as Kylo prepared to take the walk to the stage. "...Tony Scarpellini."

The applause was rapturous, the young winner trotted to the stage, took possession of his trophy and made a short and stumbling speech. Kylo, unnoticed by the whooping, cheering crowd, slipped through the door and walked quickly to the elevator and pressed the bell. Fortunately, the door slid open without delay. He stepped in quickly and this time didn't look at himself in the little mirror on the back wall.

He entered his room and slammed the door. He stood inside motionless for a moment and then strode over to the French windows and opened them to the small balcony. The sea was navy blue, with a narrow, shimmering carpet of gold where the new moon shone. The waves sounded sleepy.

"I lost," he told himself. "I bloody well lost to a bloody tennis player who never risks his life like I do." He couldn't understand his emotions, he felt numb. Sighing deeply, he closed the windows and sat on the bed, his head in his hands. He picked up his smart phone. He would call Mia.

He had known her for fourteen years, since he was eight and she was six. She had moved, with her parents, into the shack on the beach next to where he lived with his father and mother and two elder brothers. Her father, like his, was a fisherman and the two men were friends, going out to sea to fish every day. This made their friendship inevitable and, as kids, they used to play on the beach together after school.

Kylo had been twelve when a foreigner arrived on their beach with a strange craft consisting of a surf board and sail. The fishermen laughed but Kylo was fascinated as the foreigner went to sea on his craft every day, not to fish, but to have fun. He watched how the foreigner let the sail catch the breeze, sending the board skimming over the waves.

The foreigner had taught him when they were on the beach

together how to operate the windsurf board and he was ecstatic when the man took him out one day, showing him how to manoeuvre the sail and control the board. Soon afterwards, the foreigner didn't come to the beach, but his windsurf board and sail were still there.

'He left it for you,' said his father. 'He's gone back to his country.'

From that day, every spare minute he had, Kylo went windsurfing. He saw Mia only in the evenings, when they sat on the sand and watched the sunset. Kylo left school at sixteen, but Mia stayed on for further studies and he saw her less and less. For most of the day, he went fishing with his father, going back to sea on the windsurf board when fishing was over. He loved the ocean, knew its moods, and couldn't understand why Mia didn't share his enthusiasm.

'One day,' he told her as they watched the sun set, 'I will be like that foreigner and become a windsurf champion. I shall travel the world, surf with my board on every ocean.'

'What about me?' she said. 'I thought we would always be together.'

As he recalled the moment she had said that, there was a loud knock on the bedroom door.

"Kylo?" said a gruff voice. A man's voice.

Kylo sighed. It wasn't the first time someone had banged on his hotel room door at night. He ignored the knock, hoping the man would go away.

"Kylo," said the voice. "I know you're in there. I want to talk to you."

"Go away!" Kylo shouted in return. "I'm phoning my *girl*friend," he said, emphasising the word 'girl'.

"If you let me in, I'll give you some news to tell her."

Kylo was intrigued. This didn't sound like the usual fan's lament which was usually, "Kylo I'm in love with you. Let me in and I'll be yours."

He walked over to the door and looked through the peep hole. He saw the face of man with fashionable stubble on his pudgy features. He was wearing a tuxedo with a real bow tie, not a clip-on one. Kylo was puzzled. From experience, he sensed the man was not the usual hero-worshipper. He looked as though he meant business.

Keeping the safety chain on the door, Kylo opened it a few inches. "What do you want?" he said through the gap

The man looked relieved that he had answered. "Can I come in? It's all right, Kylo. I just want to talk to you. I have a proposition, a *business* proposition."

"I've heard that one before," Kylo said, preparing to close the door.

The man laughed. "I'm sure you have. Look, my name's Lex Goldberg. I produce blockbuster movies. *Beneath The Waves*, *Mermaid In Love, The Sea Monster Returns...* They're mine. Here's my card." He thrust a business card at Kylo who took it cautiously, wondering what this was about. The card gave the name of a film company and an address in Hollywood.

"Okay," said Kylo, releasing the safety catch. He felt sure he could throw the man out if he tried anything stupid. "You can come in, but only for a few minutes, understand?"

"Yes, my boy." The man stepped quickly into the room. "Shall we sit down?" He pointed to the chairs at the coffee table, not to the bed. "My flight leaves in a couple of hours, that's why this can't wait until the morning. I honestly thought you'd win tonight," he said. "From all I've heard about you, you should have done."

Kylo shrugged his shoulders. "Please, Mr Goldberg. What's this all about?"

"It's about you. I'm staying in the penthouse; came here to meet some investors in my next movie, and I heard you were here. It's only now I have a chance to catch up with you."

"And why should you want to do that?" asked Kylo, still suspicious about the man's motives in coming to his bedroom.

"My casting director has told me about you. She's shown me video clips of you windsurfing and of your physique. She says you're probably the dude we want."

"For…?"

"My next movie, of course: *Lord of the Waves*. It's a kind of Tarzan movie, set on the ocean, not in the jungle. We need a popular windsurfing star, like you, who looks damn good in Speedos. We'll have great windsurfing sequences that will thrill people, packing them in to the cinemas. Of course you'll have to come to Hollywood for a screen test, but from the videos we've seen, you're a natural for the movie."

"Hollywood?" Kylo stared at the man siting opposite him. He *seemed* genuine.

"Sure. Are you interested? My studio will make the arrangements, send you a first-class air ticket, arrange a hotel suite, meals, limousine. All your expenses will be taken care of. If the test is okay, we'll offer you a contract."

The man glanced at his gold Rolex, stood up, and held out this hand. "I've got to rush. Send me a text message saying when you can fly over."

"One question," said Kylo trying not to crush the man's hand as he shook it. "Can I bring my girlfriend?"

"Sorry, son. We like our stars to be without encumbrances. You know, fans want their idols to be unattached. They want to feel they have a chance, especially with a dude with your looks and charisma."

He walked towards the door. "Think about it, son. I'll give you three days to let me know, then get ready for Hollywood."

The room was eerily silent after the departure of Lex Goldberg. Kylo sat down on the edge of the bed, his mind in turmoil. He rarely had a drink, unless it was local island rum with friends after a day of windsurfing, but he needed something. He had a lot to think about.

Of course, it was completely out of the question to go down to the bar. He knew that guests who had been at the award ceremony would be there, holding each other up, too drunk to stand alone, still crowing with laughter at nothing in particular. They would fall silent as he walked into the room, and then crowd around him offering drinks. Instead, he rang room service and ordered a bottle of rum, a coke and some ice.

It seemed an eternity before the rum arrived, but it gave him time to think. He tipped the room service waiter, noting that he didn't ask for his autograph, and opened the bottle. Pouring himself a large measure and adding a small amount of coke, he took the glass and his thoughts to the narrow balcony and stood, staring out to sea. The waves lapped the shore, bubbling forward and hissing back again. The sound seemed to mock him.

He felt like throwing something, breaking something, hurting himself. He turned back into the room, slammed the balcony window shut and poured himself another drink, wondering where the first one had gone to so quickly. He tried to catch his breath, to make sense of what had happened.

After his third drink, his anger diminished and self-pity took its place. He wasn't used to being beaten. Having been voted Sports Personality of the Universe twice, and won so many championships during the year, he expected the title to be his.

"I'll never be able to show myself on the beaches again," he thought, almost weeping. "Someone will point and whisper, *'That's Kylo Ganoo,'* and then people will say, *'Who the hell is Kylo Ganoo?'"*

As he went to pour another drink, he spotted the card Lex Goldberg had given him lying on the coffee table. Through blurred eyes, he read it again: the address of the Goldberg Studios in Hollywood, and a phone number. It was all very strange, especially as he hadn't won that year's title. Oh yes, Kylo had heard of Lex Goldberg, everyone had heard of him. But why should Kylo be selected instead of this year's award winner? "Because," Kylo thought with a sudden rush of confidence, "because Lex Goldberg wants a windsurfer in his movie, not a wimp of a tennis player."

With his brain numbed by the rum, he tried to weigh up the pros and cons, but found that there were no cons. He reached for his smart phone and carefully, like a schoolboy doing homework, tapped out a message to Lex Goldberg, accepting his offer and asking him to arrange his ticket to fly to Hollywood from the hotel, before he went back home to his island.

#

The sun, shining through the windows where he had left the curtains open, woke him. He lay in a stupor, his head pounding, keeping his eyes closed, wondering what had happened. He wasn't at home where he still lived with his parents and brothers, and where the sun streamed into the beach shack in the morning. The bed was too comfortable. And there was no noise of children playing on the beach outside.

Gradually, he remembered. Some upstart tennis player from Europe had won the title that had been his for the past two years. The pendulum had swung, from Indian Ocean islands to the Western world. It was like the United Nations, with different continents getting a turn each year to provide the UN president.

He sat up with a start, clutching his throbbing head. First he remembered he hadn't called Mia, then he remembered why: Lex Goldberg had invited him to star in *Lord of the Waves*, if he passed the screen test. *Huh*, he thought, *screen test? Haven't they seen enough of my body riding the waves? That's a formality.*

Thoroughly awake now, he jumped out of bed, striding out to the bathroom. He plunged into a cold shower, letting the water sting his back and head, washing away the effects of the previous night's rum. As he soaped himself he glanced in the mirror, as he always did, at his naked body. His muscles gleamed under the soapy water. He was indeed at the peak of physical fitness. It reassured him and suddenly he didn't care about the stupid title. He was still three-times world champion wind surfer.

After eating breakfast in the room and feeling almost normal, he picked up his phone. There was a text from someone called Rhona saying she was replying on behalf of Lex Goldberg and would let him know flight details later that day. He chuckled to himself and entered Mia's number on the phone.

"Hello," a sleepy voice answered. "Kylo, is that you? It's three in the morning here!"

"I'm sorry, Mia. I'm on the other side of the world."

"That's where you always are, even when you're here."

"What?" He didn't understand. "How are you?"

"All right. At least I was until you woke me."

He was puzzled. "I thought you'd be pleased to hear from me?"

19

"Of course I am, Kylo. I've got wonderful news to tell you. I've been accepted at the University of Aberdeen School of Medicine. I'm going to Britain, Kylo. I'm going to be a doctor."

"What?" He paused. "I didn't know you were studying."

"Of course you did, silly. I told you last year. Perhaps you forgot. It's been a year since we met."

"That's why I'm calling." he said. "I'm going to retire from competitive windsurfing. That's for kids. We can get married."

There was silence.

"Mia, are you there. Did you hear?"

"I heard, Kylo, but did you hear me? I'm going *away* from the beach. I'm going to be a doctor."

"So?"

"Don't you see? You made your decision a year ago. You chose the sea. Now I've made mine. We can't get married, Kylo. Not now, not any when. Goodbye."

"Wait, Mia!" He was too late; the connection was broken.

2. Pearls Before Swine

They sat in their mourning attire around the Chippendale table, whilst Mr Snell, the family solicitor, read the will.

Gladys, who had been the personal servant to the Dowager Lady Pitchford-Smythe for 28 years, hovered by the sideboard, flicking flies off the plate of cold meats with the hem of her apron, and wondering when she should start pouring the sherry. She gazed at them in disdain. "Like a flock of old crows," she said to herself. There were five of them; the eldest son, Lord Cedric, and his wife, Helen; the dowager's daughter, Marjorie, and her spineless husband, Donald; and Bertie, the younger son, already tipsy.

Gladys was shocked by what Bertie was wearing for the reading of his mother's will—a smart black suit and white shirt, but sporting a cherry red tie. He looked like a mourner on a Bank Holiday.

On and on Mr Snell droned, about shares and stocks and minor bequests. The assembled family writhed in frustration, eager for him to reach the important bit - how much had Mother left them?

When she heard the final figures for each of them, and the crocodile tears had evaporated and complacent smiles taken their place, Gladys could have fainted with shock. *That much!* she thought.

"And of course," said Mr Snell, gathering the paperwork and

putting it in his briefcase, "as you are now the head of the household, Lord Pitchford-Smythe, the house and estate is now your responsibility."

Cedric beamed, but not as much as his wife did. *With the old dowager dead,* Helen thought, *I'm the only Lady Pitchford-Smythe and can run the house as I want.*

"And there's Gladys," Mr Snell continued.

At her position by the sideboard, Gladys jumped to attention, the sherry decanter at the ready.

"Who is Gladys?" asked the solicitor.

"I am, sir," she said, gently bobbing a curtsey to him.

"Ah yes, you're the maid, aren't you?"

"I was Lady Pitchford-Smythe's personal servant for twenty-eight years, sir," she replied.

"Oh," said Mr Snell. "Then you are to have the first pick from her Ladyship's jewellery collection. Apparently, the box is kept in her dressing room. Can you see to that, Lord Pitchford-Smythe?" Leaving behind a slight whiff of mothballs, the solicitor took his leave.

There was a stunned silence as the family turned in unison to stare at Gladys. "Well!" said Helen. "As I am now the only Lady Pitchford-Smythe, I really think it is I who should have the first choice of the dowager's jewels."

"Just one moment," retorted Marjorie, "I happen to be the only daughter. I am *family*, unlike some."

"Oh!" exclaimed Helen, "and what does *that* mean, pray?"

The two husbands hushed their wives, reminding them that now was *not* the time for arguments, and Bertie, lighting a cigarette, said, "Pour the sherry Gladys, there's a good girl."

#

Four of them, and Gladys, stood in awkward silence in the bedroom, aware that the bed on which Bertie was lolling was where the deceased had recently succumbed. He had already delayed the proceedings by having a second glass of sherry, while the others were eager to see the contents of the dowager's jewellery box.

"Where is the box?" asked Lord Cedric, in hushed, respectful tones.

"In the dressing room, sir," said Gladys. "I'll get it, shall I?"

It was a rather small casket, frustratingly small, disappointing Helen and Marjorie judging by their crest-fallen expressions.

"And the key?" enquired his Lordship.

"In the dressing table drawer," replied Gladys. "Top one, underneath the stockings."

The key was brought forth and the box opened. There was the sound of indrawn breath, mostly from the ladies.

"Talk about Aladdin's Cave," said Bertie with a chuckle.

"And which would you choose, Gladys?" asked Helen, praying that it wouldn't be the pearls.

"This one, if you please," replied the maid. "This brooch with the big red stone."

There were sighs of relief from Helen and Marjorie. Holding the brooch tightly in her hand, Gladys addressed Cedric. "If you please, my lord, I would like to give my notice."

"Ah, yes," he said. "Well, I am sure you have been a good and faithful servant to my mother all these years, and, er… yes. Accepted."

Well, he thought, *that's one little bit of awkwardness out of the way.* He had been wondering how to sack her, the cook and the gardeners because, although he hadn't discussed it with the family, it was his intention to sell the crumbling old house.

"And I'll just take the key to the jewellery box off you, shall I, my dear?" said Cedric. "It will be kept in my possession until we can all sit down properly and sort things out." They then left, arguing and snapping, back to the sherry in the drawing room.

"Well," said Bertie, "what will you do, Gladys?"

She stopped as she was about to follow the others downstairs and looked over at him in surprise as he got up off the bed. "Oh, I didn't know you were still here, sir."

"Where will you go?" he asked.

"To my sister," she said. "She's got a little tea shop with a flat above, in Hythe."

"And what will you do with that hideous red brooch?" he asked. "Wear it when you take the cake-stand round?"

"Oh no, sir," said Gladys. "I shall sell it."

Bertie laughed and kissed her on the cheek. "Come on, Gladys. Pack your case and I'll run you to the station."

"It's done already," she said, pointing to her case in a corner of the room. Taking one last look at the room she had got to know so well, she followed Bertie as he carried her case down the stairs.

#

Gladys was in the kitchen of her sister's tea shop, making cucumber and fish paste sandwiches as the day's special, when her sister burst into the kitchen.

"Oh, Gladys," she said. "There's a gent at the counter, asking for you. A right toff, he is. What shall I tell him?"

"Don't worry, Doris," she said with a smile. "I know how to

deal with them toffs after working with a bunch of them for years. I'll see what he wants." With a quick glance in the kitchen mirror, she smoothed down her hair, untied her apron, took a deep breath, and opened the door into the café.

She was not surprised to see Bertie standing at the other side of the counter, looking uncomfortable among the tea shop customers. His face showed his relief at seeing her. She felt amused, but wouldn't let it show.

"Oh, Gladys," he said, almost shouting with delight. "I'm so glad I've found you. I've been drinking tea in every tea shop in Hythe looking for you. I'm sure I'll never want a cup of tea again."

"Then I won't offer you one," she said, with a smile. "I know tea's not your cup of tea, anyway."

"What? Oh yes. I suppose you don't have any sherry hidden away in this place. In your room, perhaps?"

"Of course not," she said, treating Bertie as though he were still a little boy. He was four years old when she began to work for his mother. She had watched him grow up, seeing him asserting his independence and individuality as he grew older. Gladys looked at him shrewdly. He seemed to have lost his rakish charm since she had last seen him when he had dropped her at the station after she handed in her notice.

He saw her appraising him. "Things have changed since mother died," he said, without her asking anything. "My brother's wife, Helen, rules the roost now. Or thinks she does. Cedric wants to sell the house and the estate."

"But your family has lived there for centuries." Gladys was shocked. "Why does he want to sell? Your mother left plenty of money."

Bertie glanced around the café anxiously. "Is there

somewhere we can talk, Gladys?"

"Come to the back," she said, holding up the counter flap for him to pass through. "We have a sitting room in the back. That's where I take my break."

He followed her into the kitchen. "This is my sister, Doris," Gladys said, pointing at the woman in the kitchen.

"How do you do?" Bertie held out his hand at which Doris giggled, but didn't shake it.

"He wants to have a talk, Doris. We going to the sitting room."

Gladys opened the sitting room door for Bertie and showed him to a chair.

He sat down cautiously. "How are you keeping, Gladys? I miss you around the old place." He paused. "Still have that ghastly brooch?"

She looked at him, her face expressionless. "I might have."

"Don't worry, Gladys. You can trust me. Just wondered if you'd found a buyer for that awful thing."

"Awful, is it?" There was silence.

Bertie scratched his head and sighed. "I have to be honest with you, Gladys. All that money Mother thought she had to leave to us. There's nothing. So many debts, failed investments by my father and Cedric too. Most of it went on gambling. Even mother's jewellery turned out to be fake."

He paused. "I wondered why you picked that brooch, Gladys, out of all that jewellery. Did you know its value?

Gladys sniffed. "I liked it," she said. "It was your mother's favourite. She said it was a ruby. Is it fake too?"

Bertie smiled with relief. "Ah, that means you haven't sold it. It's real all right, Gladys. I had a hunch about that brooch. I've been checking. The gem isn't fake, it's a large pigeon blood red ruby, very rare, very valuable. Been in my mother's family since the seventeenth century. It's so valuable and famous, it even has a name. The ruby is called the Ceylonese Princess." He stood up, his smile giving way to a stern stare.

"May I see it, Gladys? To remind me of my mother."

"Oh no," she said. "It's somewhere safe where neither you, nor your brother, nor sister, nor their gold-digging spouses can get it. The brooch is mine. I earned it, devoting my life to your mother, being at her beck and call night and day, slaving for you all for a pittance for twenty-eight years."

Bertie stared at her in amazement. "Gladys!" he said, "I've never heard you speak like this before! Have we really been that awful?"

"I would not wish the lot of you onto my worst enemy, Master Bertie," she retorted.

"Master Bertie?" he smiled wryly. "You haven't called me that since I was a little boy."

"And you've never grown up," retorted Gladys. "A nasty little child you were then, a spiteful, snivelling brat who told lies and stole from my room and probably from the rest of your family. And you haven't changed, Master Bertie, not one bit."

Bertie had the grace to blush. "I really am in hot water, Gladys," he said. "We *all* are. If Cedric manages to sell that draughty old house, there wouldn't be much money left over for the family, not after death duties."

"Why have you come to see me, Master Bertie?" she asked. "If it is the brooch you are after, then the answer is no. And if you think I will sell it and give you some of the money I make, you must think I was born yesterday!"

"No, Gladys," he replied eagerly, "but I do know someone who would give you a magnificent sum for the brooch, and I was thinking, well, a sort of… er… commission on the sale."

Gladys laughed out loud. "You must be joking."

Bertie hung his head, shuffled his feet and pouted his lips. He looked about four years old at that moment.

Gladys patted his arm. "Why do you think your mother put that red brooch on the very top of the fake jewels? I'll tell you why—it was because she wanted me to have it! Now, off you go and sort your problems out. Please don't come back and see me, because the Pitchford-Smythes and I have parted company." She opened the door to show Bertie out of the sitting room. He went without another word, shaking his head sadly.

\#

Lord Pitchford-Smythe sat at the head of the antique Chippendale table with its stylised legs and feet. He was used to convening estate meetings, but not a family one like this. "Order," he said loudly, banging his gavel, which was quite unnecessary as the four other members present were his family and too depressed and bewildered to cause an uproar.

"Are we all present and correct?" he demanded.

"Oh, get on with it, do," snapped his wife, Lady Helen. "Of course we're all here!"

Rising to his feet, Cedric addressed the gathering pompously. "Firstly," he began, and was immediately interrupted by Bertie.

"Can't we start with *lastly*, Cedric?"

"Order," he muttered miserably, suddenly losing confidence, "*Firstly*," he repeated, trying to recover his poise, glaring at his younger brother. He paused. "Oh, what the bloody hell are we going to do?" he said in despair, and sat down.

Bertie gazed around the table. *Old Gladys was right*, he thought to himself. *What a lot of nasty individuals we are. There isn't one decent soul amongst us, what with our secrets and vices and underhand dealings. It's a miracle the lot of us haven't been arrested and banged up years ago! Look at Marjorie, that sister of mine! Wiping her eyes every time our mother's name is mentioned, but ransacking her wardrobe to get to the sable and mink before Helen got a look in. And as for her husband, old Donald. He looks frightened half to death. I wonder what he's got to be scared of?*

And dear Helen, thinking she can really take my mother's place as head of the household. Where does she really go, he wondered, *when she's supposedly booked in at a health farm? And Cedric, my brother, good old Lord Cedric. Something has really rattled his apple-cart. Guilty,* he decided. *They all look guilty. And desperate. And scared bloody witless. And what about me?* he agonised. *Oh my God, what the hell am I to do? What about me?*

Cedric, banging the gavel pointedly, roused him from his thoughts.

"Bertie," he said "please pay attention. "I have called this meeting to give you all some bad news."

"More?" Donald asked. "What can be worse than to know that all your mother's bequests are worthless?"

"There is something," Cedric said. "I planned to sell the house and estate."

"That's good," said his sister. "I never liked this old dump anyway. Gives me the creeps."

"Sell!" exclaimed his wife, clutching her bosom as though she were about to faint. "What? I only married you because you said one day this would be mine. Now your mother's dead, this is *my* home."

"Technically," said Bertie deliberately trying to rile her. "It's only your home if Cedric wishes."

"What's this all about?" asked Donald. "You said *planned* to sell. That seems sensible. We as family could all have our shares, to make up for those worthless bequests."

"And being left fake jewellery," said his wife.

"The ruby brooch isn't a fake. The one Gladys chose from the box. It's famous. The Ceylonese Princess, it's called. Worth millions." Bertie smiled at their distress.

"Millions?" Cedric's voice squeaked as he looked at his younger brother in surprise. "How did she choose that? The only gem that wasn't fake."

"She says it's what mother wanted." Bertie shrugged his shoulders.

"But what about this house, and the estate?" asked Donald again.

"That's the problem." Cedric sighed. "I asked Snell, the solicitor chappie engaged by mother, about selling it. It appears I cannot, even though it's mine on her death."

"Why ever not?" said Donald.

"It's entailed. It can only ever be inherited and owned by the son or heir of Lord Pitchford-Smythe. Mother was keeping it in trust for me."

"But you don't have any children to inherit," Marjorie said quickly. "We do."

"Yes," said Donald sitting up. "Two boys."

"But they are not Pitchford-Smythes," said Cedric.

"Well, that's true for sure." Bertie smothered a laugh with his hand.

"Perhaps you could adopt one of my sons," said Marjorie to

Cedric. "They're both family blood through me."

"Or you could father a son yourself," said Bertie with a laugh and a wicked grin at Helen. "Or is one of you sterile? I often wondered why you never gave him a son, Helen. Of course, I should be grateful. Since Cedric has no son, that makes me my brother's heir.

"You mean our house will go to you?" His sister was almost in tears. "That's not fair."

"Why not?" asked Bertie, enjoying taunting the others. "I was always mother's favourite."

"What rot!" Marjorie almost spat at him. "She loathed you for your philandering. You never had a job, never contributed anything to this family."

"What about you, dear sister? How many lovers have you had behind Donald's back? Are your children even his? Your affairs don't exactly enhance the family name."

"Lovers? Affairs?" Donald turned to his wife. "Is that true, Marjorie?"

Cedric banged the table so hard with his gavel, it wobbled, its antique legs almost collapsing. "Meeting's adjourned," he said. "Somehow we have to find a solution, or else it's the poor house for all of us."

#

Gladys felt the sun on her face, and manoeuvred her body into a more comfortable position on the sun lounger. The private beach which was connected to her hotel by a narrow flight of steps was almost silent. It was siesta time. Just the soothing sound of the lap of wavelets kissing the edge of the sand, and the distant sound of music coming from a small party further along the beach. A

31

shadow blocked the sun. She smiled up at the young Italian waiter standing beside her and accepted a Campari from his tray of drinks.

"My goodness," she chuckled to herself, "there's life in the old girl yet." She closed her eyes and let her thoughts sort themselves. Of course, the Ceylonese Princess brooch was far away, out of the grasping hands of the Pitchford-Smythes. It was the first piece of jewellery Gladys had sold.

She recalled with a smile those cosy, intimate evenings she had spent in the dear old dowager's bed chamber during her last illness. Talking and planning. Drinking sherry and giggling like schoolgirls.

It had been the dowager's wish that Gladys should have her collection of jewellery. She had made the decision when she realised what a useless bunch her children were, just like their wastrel father.

What a surprise they would have when the will was read. For the first time in their lives, they would have to work, instead of sponging off her and the wealth she had brought from her own inheritance when she married.

She had told Gladys to bring the jewel box from the dressing room. Gladys had unlocked it as she instructed and the contents were tipped onto the counterpane of her bed. The sight was dazzling. One by one, as the dowager watched, the treasures were wrapped in stockings, knickers, petticoats, gloves, scarves, and packed at the bottom of a suitcase that belonged to Gladys and covered with Gladys's clothes. It was this very suitcase which Bertie himself had carried downstairs for Gladys when she left.

Then came the next part of the dowager's cunning plan. She already had replicas, paste copies, of all her jewellery. They were very good likenesses that fooled everybody when she wore them.

The priceless Ceylonese Princess ruby was the most important part of the treasury since she had never trusted any jeweller to make a copy, and the only worrying part of the planned procedure.

Gladys watched as her old friend filled the box and placed the brooch on top of the make-believe pieces, and winked at her. The dowager told Gladys she would make sure that nobody else had first pick of the jewels when the will was read.

The dowager gave her a slip of paper which, to Gladys, was almost as valuable as the brooch in the jewel box. It was a list of people on the Continent who would gladly purchase the jewellery. This would mean Gladys would have to travel around Europe, but, at the age of seventy, she felt quite ready for the adventure which lay ahead.

The Ceylonese Princess ruby was sold within two minutes of Gladys entering the little shop in Soho. The amount of money that was paid into her newly opened bank account was astounding. She was able to buy a small hotel for Doris to run on the sea front at Hythe and to sell the tea shop.

#

Siesta seemed to be at an end. People were making their way from the hotel to the beach, bagging sunbeds and erecting sun umbrellas. The Italian waiter hovered near by, and Gladys accepted another Campari.

That morning she had been into the town at Tuscany and sold the pair of emerald earrings and a diamond-studded bangle. As the sun caressed her face, she felt fulfilled and complacent, having done what the dowager wanted. Tomorrow she would sell the pearls.

3. The Sand Castle

"Why should a grown man want to build a sand castle?" asked John's wife when he announced he was going to enter the resort's Sand Castle competition.

"Why not?" he said. "There are hundreds of adults who do. They have competitions in the USA and Australia and there's a World Sand Sculpting Academy promoting the art."

"But we're here on holiday," Alice said from her deckchair. "It sounds childish to me."

John didn't answer. When he was a boy with a bucket and spade during a family holiday at Torquay, he spent all his time on the beach building sand castles. He used to add a moat around the small castle of bucket-pie towers and watch as the sea splashed in and filled the moat with water. He would spend hours shovelling and piling sand into different shapes, only to have the tide come in and wash away his castle. He didn't mind; he had created something lovely.

The chance to enter the hotel's weekly castle building competition for guests during their holiday by the beach, was too good to miss. The hotel's animator said the competition was open to everyone, not just children, and to locals as well as hotel guests.

"What will I do while you're playing at being a kid again?" Alice asked, after he had signed up for the contest being held the next day.

"Relax on the beach, write postcards and enjoy the sun like we've been doing since we've been here," John said. "Only another three days before we fly home. You can take photographs too."

Alice sighed. She began to wonder if the sand castle competition that was promoted on its website as one of the resort's activities was why John had chosen the hotel. She didn't really mind, if he was happy. It was the first holiday they had had together without their children since their honeymoon. They had swum and sunbathed on the beach all day, gorged themselves on the buffets at breakfast, lunch and dinner, and enjoyed the magic show, the cultural dancing, and the bingo in the evenings. They had been on a boat ride on the river, a jeep safari to view wild elephants, had a tour of the tea plantations in the hill country and climbed the huge natural monolith of granite, with its ruined fortress at the summit and water gardens at its base, called the Lion Rock. It had been their best holiday ever.

"It starts after breakfast," he said.

"You didn't bring your bucket and spade," Alice said with a laugh. "You'll be disqualified."

"The organisers provide them in return for the registration fee. It only costs ten dollars, the same price as a couple of cocktails. The prize is a magnum of champagne in an ice bucket for adults and a bucket of ice-cream for kids."

"The champagne's yours," Alice said. "You'll be the only adult there."

Alice was wrong. She and John were both surprised to see there were a dozen adults gathered at eight o'clock the next morning on the beach, with about twenty kids.

John went to the desk to register. "Where's your team mate?" asked the hotel's animator.

John was flummoxed. "I don't have one."

"There must be at least two people in each team."

John looked along the beach. Alice had already settled in a deckchair and started writing postcards so he couldn't ask her. He doubted if she would help anyway.

"Sir?"

He turned to his right side where a bronzed youth wearing only beach shorts was looking at him hopefully. "If you need someone to help, I'll do so. I can dig and carry the sand."

John hesitated. "My wife might help…"

"I've done it before."

"Well, yes, why not? Thanks." He turned back to the registration desk. "Is it all right?"

The animator nodded.

What's your name?" John asked the boy.

"Lal." The lad grinned and took up an industrial-size bucket and spade from the pile by the desk.

"Okay. We're John and Lal," said John.

"Team name?" asked the animator.

"Rock stars," said Lal quickly, as John hesitated.

"You start when the whistle blows. Any building design you like. You have two hours and must stop when the whistle blows again. Yours is Plot Number Seven."

They walked together to where the beach was flat and the sand wet from the receding tide. Fifteen plots identified by numbers on a flag were marked out on the beach. They found Plot Number Seven.

"Two hours doesn't seem much time," John said to Lal.

Lal shrugged his shoulders. "It's all we've got."

"Okay," said John. "We need to collect a pile of sand. We'll build a castle with ramparts and turrets at the corners and a keep—that's a tower—in the centre, and a moat all around the castle for the sea to fill." With the edge of his spade John marked the outline of his planned castle.

"No, no," said Lal, rubbing the indents out with his bare foot. "We don't need a European castle. Let's be different. We'll make a replica of the Lion Rock, with battlements around a tower on the top and water gardens below, instead of a moat."

"I've been to the Lion Rock," said John. "It's about 350 feet high towering up over flat scrub land with a couple of acres of a ruined citadel at the top."

"So we need lots of wet sand to build it to scale," said Lal. "Take the bucket and go and dig and carry as much as you can."

"Now hang on a minute!" John, annoyed, but smiling at the novel idea the youth was suggesting. "This is *my* sand castle, remember!"

Alice, who had drawn up her deckchair to be nearer the pair, smiled and said, "Now, now, children. You're a team. Play nicely." She returned to writing her postcards.

The whistle blew. Lal grabbed the bucket impatiently and dashed off to collect damp sand from where the surf was washing the beach.

John suddenly had a thought. "Those postcards," he said, walking over to Alice. "Let me see them."

"Why?" Alice handed them over. "You want to see what I've written?"

"No," said John. "I can guess that." He looked at them quickly. "I'm right. All you've written is 'Wish you were here.' What you really mean is 'Look where I am.'" He shuffled hurriedly through the postcards looking at the pictures.

Lal ran over with a bucket of sand which he emptied onto their plot. "Please, sir. Stop reading the postcards and start piling up the sand."

John looked at him in amazement at being ordered what to do by a kid who seemed to be the same age as his eldest son. Alice giggled. Lal ran back for more sand.

"Ah!" said John, pulling out a postcard from the pack and handing the rest back to Alice. "Here's a postcard of the Lion Rock. I see it has steps up the side to a ledge with two lions carved out of rock guarding the entrance."

Lal returned and tipped out more sand. John took the bucket from his hand. "I'll carry the sand," he said, handing him the postcard. "Here's what we're going to build."

Lal's smile was dazzling. "Yes, sir!" he said happily as he began to shape the pile of sand to resemble a giant mushroom protruding from a desert plain.

John ran backwards and forwards bringing more sand. He was surprised to see a crowd of curious spectators gathering around the red flags which defined their plot.

"Do you have a pocket knife, sir?" Lal asked.

John, running out of breath after carrying so much sand, sank to his knees beside Alice's deckchair. He shook his head.

"I need something to carve the lions and steps up the side," said Lal.

"Will my nail clippers help?" said Alice, digging into her handbag.

Lal grabbed them. "You do the ruined castle with battlements at the top," he told John. "I'll carve out the staircase and sculpt the lions at the gate. You dig the water gardens and fashion palm trees around the base of the tower."

John shook his head in shock at being told what to do.

"Hurry," said Lal, "We have less than an hour to finish."

John obeyed, giving way to the excitement bubbling up

inside his chest as he began to dig ditches for the water garden which the incoming tide would fill. He used the discarded sand to mould into palm trees.

The two worked together in silent concentration, while Alice watched with pride at what her husband was doing and the bond that was building up between him and Lal. She thought of their two sons, and how surprised they would be to see their Dad enjoying himself on the beach like a child.

A whistle blew. Time was up. Alice got up from the deckchair and reached in her bag for her camera to take a photograph of the beautiful, tall sand castle with two realistically modelled lions that they had built. "John, stand beside Lal with your hand on his shoulder," she said. She looked through the viewfinder, but Lal was nowhere to be seen. He had slipped away and disappeared into the crowd.

#

"Oh *do* come in from the balcony, John," begged Alice. "Surely the tide has taken all the castles away by now."

"Not mine," announced John proudly. "I can see the tower is still standing with the battlements on top. The sea has filled the water gardens I made. It's lovely."

"Well, it'll be gone soon, so let's have another glass of champagne before we go for lunch." Slightly tiddly, she giggled. "Fancy you winning this huge bottle of champagne! I wish we could take some back home to show the boys when they come to get their presents and look at our holiday snaps."

"We'll take the cork back," said John, still gazing at the outline of his tower, so soon to be covered by the incoming tide. Of the other pathetic sand castle efforts there was no sign; they had been completely washed away.

"I wonder where on earth Lal disappeared to," mused Alice. "He should have been here with us, sharing the prize. He seemed such a nice young man."

"A bit bossy, I thought," John said, closing the balcony doors. "It's gone." He sounded sad. "My castle has gone."

"Your castle?" Alice said. "It's was the boy's idea." She reached over and patted his hand.

John drew back. "It was your camera that did it."

"*What* was my camera?"

"When you started pointing the camera at him, he took off like a frightened rabbit. I wonder why."

After an enormous buffet lunch, they had a siesta in the room. John was tired after so much activity in the morning, while Alice felt the effects of too much champagne. After his rest, John decided to go for a walk on the beach.

"You go alone," Alice said. "I know you want to see the ruin of your castle."

"I might see Lal," he said. "I never even thanked him for his help. And his idea."

The tide had come in, almost to the grass verge that bordered the beach, and there was nothing remaining of the morning's sand castles. It made John reflect on the temporary nature of everything, including his unexpected relationship with Lal, a boy he didn't even know but whose instructions and commands he followed in the building of the castle. He wasn't used to taking orders from anyone, especially a teenage boy on the beach.

He wondered where Lal had come from, where he had gone, and whether he would ever see him again. He had been impressed by the boy's confidence, as well as his talent in sculpting the lions and steps with Alice's nail clippers.

He was pleased to see the hotel's animator was walking towards him, carrying the folding table he had used when he registered participants. "Excuse me," said John as they met. "May I ask you something?"

"Good afternoon, Mr John," said the man, pausing and putting down the table. "How can I help?"

"I was wondering," said John, "if you know anything about Lal, my team mate building the castle."

"Has he stolen anything from you, sir?"

"Oh no," said John. "Why should you think that?"

"He's a bad egg, sir. Always hanging around our tourists."

"He's very talented, the way he sculpted that sand rock we built."

"I thought you did that, sir."

"No. It was all his idea, He disappeared before the prize giving. He doesn't even know we won."

"Don't worry about him, sir. You're lucky he didn't ask you for money. That's what they all do."

John frowned. 'Do you know him personally?"

"Well, no." The animator picked up his table. "I must be going, sir."

John watched him walk back to the hotel. He was puzzled, wondering if the animator was lying. He had found Lal, apart from his surprising air of authority, an amenable chap. Far more gumption and initiative than his own two teenage sons ever showed at home. And he had a natural creative talent. He shrugged, dismissing Lal from his mind as he continued his walk along the beach, heading for the palm grove at the corner of the bay, where he knew there was a beach shack bar selling cold beers.

"Hello, sir." A boy got up from where he was sitting in the

shade by the shack. "Beer?"

"Yes, please," said John.

The boy reached into an ice box and produced a can of cold beer which he opened and handed to John. "Wife not with you, sir?" he said, to make conversation. John shook his head. "I saw you and Lal won the sand castle contest. Lal always wins."

John sat at the beach table, sipping his beer. The feeling of euphoria that he'd experienced that morning when the judges had chosen his sandcastle as the winner, and a red flag had been placed on the top of the tall tower representing the Lion Rock, was diminishing. He tried to cling to it. He'd never won anything in his life before. The sound of applause from the onlooking crowd he could still hear in his mind. A chap from the hotel had taken his photograph, and this had been hastily printed and now stood, framed, on the reception desk. He'd had his moment of fame, and boy, he'd enjoyed it! But who, and where, was the mysterious Lal?

John felt fidgety and restless. He had expected people, as he passed them on the beach, to point and smile at him and to remark to their companions: 'That's the chap who built that fantastic sand castle this morning. With that young local lad.' *The young local lad! The missing Lal.*

John phoned his wife on his smart phone. Alice replied sleepily that she had enjoyed a wonderful rest, and was planning to walk to the town and buy gifts to take home. "Enjoy your stroll, dear," she said. "See you for dinner."

"Another beer, sir?"

"Er, no thanks." John glanced up at the boy from the shack. "Do you know Lal?" he asked. "You said he always wins."

"He does. He won the sand castle competition at the hotel at the other end of the bay yesterday."

"Does he live around here?"

"In the village, down that path." The boy pointed to a track leading through the palm trees. "His house is about a quarter of a mile down on the right. It's the only one with a palm thatch roof. All the others have proper roofs with tiles."

John nodded his thanks, paid for the beer, and got up. "I think I'll go and see him."

"I'm not sure he'll be home," said the boy. "He might be at school."

John smiled his thanks and set off along the sandy path, surprised at the news that Lal was a schoolboy. He passed several smart-looking houses, all of which were quiet at that time of the afternoon. Even the dogs lying in the shade beside the path seemed too lazy to bother with him. He was feeling hot and wished he had brought a bottle of water. For a moment, he wondered why he was looking for Lal. Of course, he wanted to thank him but he was also curious about the boy.

The house with a palm thatch roof seemed to be a temporary construction. There were sheets of galvanise tin forming one wall while the other walls were made of unplastered concrete blocks. Chickens were scratching in the sandy soil and there was a well with a bucket beside it. The bucket reminded John of the one he had carried collecting sand to build the castle.

"Lal," he called outside the front door, which was open but with the interior shielded from view by an old bed sheet serving as a curtain. "Lal?"

There was no answer but he sensed movement inside the small house. "Lal," he called again. "It's me. Your partner this morning building the Lion Rock sand castle."

The curtain was suddenly pulled aside and a small woman, probably John's age but with a wizened face like a prune making her look older, stared up at him. "At school," the woman said with a vague wave along the path. She let the curtain fall in front of his face, dismissing him.

"I'm sorry to bother you," John shouted. "I'm a friend, that's all. I want to thank him. Give him some money as his share of the prize."

As he expected, the mention of money had the desired result. The woman pulled open the curtain again. "He's got no money," she said. "He spends all he earns on the children, buying crayons and things."

John stared at her. "I don't want money," he said. "I have money to give him. What do you mean by 'earns'? I thought he was a school boy. He's got children?"

The woman laughed, her face relaxing, swelling with a hint of pride. "He's a teacher. At the play school. Teaches the children art and modelling. Like his father. Come in, I'll show you."

John stepped inside onto a sand floor. He peered into the gloom and, as the woman opened a wooden shutter, flooding the room with light, he gasped. There were clay models, of castles, of mansions, of ships and even one of the Eiffel Tower. There were also some statues, including one of a woman.

"That's you?" said John with a smile.

"When I was younger," she said coyly.

"I had no idea he is so talented," said John. "He's a natural sculptor."

"Thank you!" a voice said from the doorway. "I'm glad you like my work."

John turned to see Lal grinning at him. "Sorry I had to dash off yesterday, I had a class of kids to take care of. I heard I won."

John shook his head in disbelief. He had thought it was his own effort that had won the prize, not Lal's. He wiped his brow.

"Sorry, sir, we can't offer you anything to drink, except well water. You wouldn't like that."

"We're poor, you see," said the woman. "My son doesn't earn much and what he does goes on his sculpting. It's the only thing his dad left him."

"Hush, mam," Lal said, hugging his mother. "Don't worry about her, sir. We manage okay."

John reached for his wallet and quickly extracted a five-hundred dollar bill, all he had with him. "Take this," he said, "your share of the prize."

The woman reached for it eagerly. Lal gestured to John to let her have it. "She'll make sure I don't spend it on the children."

After a few pleasantries, John said goodbye and left the house, feeling ashamed that he couldn't do more for Lal and his mother, at least to help them finish building their house. As he reached the path, he stopped. *Of course I can do more*, he thought suddenly. *I can send him money. But I need his address so I can contact him.*

He turned back to the house and was about to go in, when he heard Lal's voice saying with a loud laugh. "You see, mam, another sucker! I'll keep on building sand castles on the beach to trap the tourists. We must never finish building this old house, though. With it looking like this, people feel sorry for us. And give us money."

4. Inheritance

It was the first time Alan had seen his son naked. Of course, he had seen the boy in Karen's arms, swaddled in baby clothes, soon after he was born. He had been late getting to the maternity home then, because of work. Although he was the owner of the printing company, he didn't like to set a bad example to his employees by dashing off when there was work to do.

Karen looked a bit peeved when he did turn up but he ignored that, taking the bundle containing his child and making the stupid noises a first-time father does. It was a miracle, and because of him.

He had dashed back to the office, paid regular visits to Karen and his son, and asked his father to take Karen back to their apartment when she and the baby were discharged from the maternity home, as he had a meeting with his accountant that day.

The boy must have been six weeks old when Alan happened to be at home, and Karen was gently bathing him. He stood at the open bathroom door and watched in astonishment. When he had first seen the boy, he was pink. Now he looked sort of sallow. Even his tiny penis and testicles were dark.

"Have you decided what to call him?" asked Karen, more to make conversation than anything else. She had already decided on Leo.

"Er, no…" Alan frowned. "I haven't had time to think of that. "Robert?" he suggested, after his father.

"Isn't that boring?" said Karen, as she dried the boy.

"You think my father's boring?

"Oh no," she said quickly, not wanting yet another argument. "He's utterly charming. What I meant was perhaps we should give baby an independent name, you know, so he doesn't feel bound by family tradition."

"Something wrong with my family tradition?" Alan was sensitive about his parents since he never knew his mother, as she died in a car accident soon after he was born. His father and his father's second wife had raised him.

"Of course not," Karen said with a sigh. "Let's give him a name that means something. I like Leo."

"Leo?"

"Yes, you know, like Leo DiCaprio."

"You want to name my son after a film star?"

"No! That's an example. After a lion. Let him be lionhearted. Like you," she said.

"Hm," he grunted. "Oh well, if you like." He looked at the naked baby again. "Isn't he a bit dark?"

"What?" She didn't understand.

"He's not very fair, is he? Do you have Italian blood in you?"

"What?"

"I mean the name you like, Leo. Italian isn't it? People might think my son's Italian."

"Don't be silly," she said. "He's going to be tall, dark and handsome... just like his father." She moved in, kissed him, and he felt ashamed.

He left the apartment soon afterwards as he had to drive back to the office. As he waited in the hallway for the lift, the building's caretaker walked past.

"Good evening, sir," the young man said.

"Good evening, Pedro," Alan replied automatically. Then he looked at the caretaker again. He was a swarthy chap, obviously a foreigner. "Hey, Pedro," he said. "Where are you from?"

"Spain, sir," said Pedro cheerfully.

The lift arrived, the door slid open and Alan entered. *Spain?* he thought. *No... She wouldn't.* He put the suspicion that had sneaked into his mind aside. *That's nonsense.* He punched the button for the basement floor where his Volvo was parked.

#

Karen finished feeding the baby and tucked her breast back into the folds of her dressing gown. She stood and, cradling the infant in her arms, gazed through the window at the scene below her.

"Over there, between those trees, is the park," she said. "We shall go there, and I will show you the pond with the ducks, and the children on the swings."

She lifted his tiny body higher, so that his eyes were in a level line with her own. "And that big, big building, the one bigger than all the others; that is Daddy's office and factory. He owns it, you know."

She continued her one-way conversation with the baby. "If we stand on tip-toe we can just see the top of the railway station. That is where Daddy gets the train when he goes away for meetings. Sometimes he gets a plane, but we can't see the airport from here."

She moved away from the window and sat in the nursing chair, which was a present from her grateful father-in-law, a thank you for the gift of his first grandchild.

She held the baby loosely in her arms, and they gazed at each other. "He is often away for long periods of time," she told him, addressing him as she would an adult. "And sometimes he gets cross and shouts." The baby burped, made little kissing sounds with his lips, and closed his eyes.

"Sorry to be such a bore," she said, but she was smiling. As she lay the precious child in his cot, and tucked the snowy fleece around him, she stared down at the miracle, the living, breathing perfection that was her baby. "He wanted to call you Robert," she whispered. "But you're my Leo."

#

It was late, very late when Alan came home. Karen was sitting in the nursing chair when he entered the apartment. She was playing with a blue velvet rabbit which a well-wisher had given the baby as a gift, caressing the long ears and plaiting the silver whiskers.

"I thought you'd be in bed," said her husband.

"You didn't phone," she replied.

"For goodness' sake," he retorted, "I've been to the most difficult and mind-blowingly boring meeting and I'm tired. The last thing I need right now is a row, but what I *do* need is a bloody drink!" He moved to the cocktail bar and poured himself a very large Scotch.

"Could I please have one?" she asked.

He stared hard at her. "Are you completely mad? You're breastfeeding my son! What sort of mother are you?"

"A very sad one," she replied.

Later, as they lay together in bed, apart and silent, Alan suddenly remarked, "Oh, by the way, I went out for an hour this afternoon to register the baby."

Karen sat up, all thoughts of sleep rushing from her. "Without me?" she asked.

49

"There is no rule about both parents being present," he said, and turned over on his side, with his back to her. Into the silence, he told her, "He is registered as Robert."

She didn't know what to say. He was acting as though she had no part in the baby. He wasn't always so contrary. She guessed something about his business must be troubling him. She reached out to touch him. "That's nice," she said. "Your father will be pleased."

"What about you? Are you pleased? Or do you still want some fancy name for the child, like Pedro, perhaps?" He moved away from her touch.

"Pedro?" She was puzzled.

"Yes, you know. Like the caretaker. His name is Pedro."

"Is it? I didn't know." She lay beside him, feeling the weight of his silence.

He must have felt it too, because he suddenly turned to her in the dark. "Oh, Karen," he said. "What's happening to us?"

"Are you under pressure at work?" she asked, reaching for him again. She squeezed his hand and felt him squeeze her hand in response. "I love you," she said. "You will tell me if something's wrong, won't you?"

"Nothing's wrong. And I registered our son's name in full as Robert Leo," he said. "That's on the birth certificate. I asked Dad and he said that would be okay."

She didn't know whether to feel pleased he had accepted her suggestion, or disappointed that he had sought his father's permission and not hers. She felt him edging towards her. Then he stopped as the baby, their son, Robert Leo, began to cry.

"We'll have to get a nurse," he said angrily, as Karen switched on the bedside lamp and got out of bed to hold the baby. "I can't be disturbed like this every night."

"Hush, hush," she said, to comfort the child. "You're keeping Daddy awake."

Alan stared at her. "I'll sleep in the spare room," he said, throwing back the covers and without bothering to put on a dressing gown over his pyjamas, padded swiftly out of the bedroom. He was puzzled. He had looked forward so much to becoming a father and was thrilled when Karen's scan revealed he was going to have a son. He had such plans for his boy. He would come into the family printing business that his father had started. But now the boy was born, the dream seemed to be falling apart.

Why had Karen wanted to call him by such a strange name? It was his father who told him to go ahead and give him the name Leo if she wanted. "The boy's her son, too," his father had told him.

Alan agreed, as he always did when his father suggested something. He had only married Karen, who was his childhood sweetheart, because his father suggested that he should settle down and she would make a good wife, being the daughter of a fellow member of the golf club where he and his father played regularly.

The marriage seemed to be going well, and Alan understood Karen might feel neglected at times while she was alone in the apartment when he was away on business trips. He had hoped the baby's arrival, after they tried so long to have a child, would be company for her.

He thought a lot about Karen and his son during the next four days, when he was out of the country on a promotion trip. He blamed himself for the gulf that had arisen between them. He resolved when he returned home he would take her and the baby away for a holiday. Somewhere they could enjoy time together as a family.

He was keen to tell her his plan as soon as he got back from the airport. He parked the Volvo, gathered the flowers he had bought her into his arms, picked up his bag, and walked to the lift, pressing the button for it.

He saw the lift was on the penthouse floor, where they lived. He waited patiently, watching the floor numbers light up as it descended. It didn't stop anywhere. He was ready to step in as the lift arrived.

"Good evening, sir." The caretaker got out of the lift as the doors opened. "May I help you, sir?" He reached out to take the bouquet from Alan's hands.

"Pedro?" Alan clutched the bouquet firmly to his chest. "No. No thanks."

"Are you okay, sir? Your wife is expecting you. I just took the mail to your apartment."

Alan stepped into the lift, pressed the button to the penthouse floor, and looked askance at Pedro as the doors closed.

#

Karen had taken nearly all the afternoon to beautify herself in preparation for Alan's return. Her hairdresser had visited, and now her crowning glory, the daffodil blonde tresses that had once made Alan weak at the knees, was a haze of soft curls, with tendrils brushing her cheeks.

She had gone with the baby to the chemist shop on the corner, his tiny body close to hers, heart to heart in the baby carrier she wore like a back-to-front rucksack. She had purchased powder, rouge, lipstick, false eye lashes. She knew she had let herself go after the birth of the baby. *Perhaps my appearance had something to do with Alan's strange mood?* she had wondered.

She decided to wear her cornflower blue gypsy skirt, ankle length and Indian cotton. And a tight little embroidered bodice. And bare feet, the way she used to dress before they were married. Looking at herself in the full-length mirror she was happy with what she saw. Surely her husband would be, too.

She heard his key in the door and quickly adopted what she hoped to be a seductive pose—half reclining on the sofa, legs tucked under her, glass of wine in her hand and a second glass awaiting him on the coffee table beside her.

Alan stepped towards her, holding out the bouquet then suddenly halted. He stared at his wife, his face darkening like thunder. He threw his case into the corner of the room, knocking a vase of flowers to the floor. Karen watched, horrified, as the water from the vase began seeping into the cream carpet.

He tossed the bouquet he held in his hands onto the sofa beside her. She flinched as he bent down and brought his face close to hers. "All dressed up?" he said with a sneer. "Didn't you expect me home so early? Have I ruined your plans for the evening?"

He looked dreadful, and Karen was afraid. "Alan, I really don't know what you are talking about. Please don't shout, you'll wake the baby."

"The baby?" he snarled. "Robert Leo—or should I say Leo Robert!"

"Alan, you are frightening me," she sobbed. "What's the matter? What have I done wrong? Look, sit down and drink the wine I've got ready for you, and I'll go and prepare lunch. I've got some cold chicken and salad and..."

"I ate on the plane," he said. "And I shall sleep at the club tonight."

She grabbed hold of the sleeve of his coat, but he shrugged her off roughly.

"Ah, I see we have mail." He walked to the sideboard and picked up the envelopes. "Did you fetch this up yourself?"

"No," she replied, "that caretaker chap, that, what's his name, er—Pedro. He brought it up."

"And did he like your pretty blue skirt, and your tight little top, and the line of your bosom, and your yellow curls? Did he?" Alan was shouting by now, and from the bedroom the baby began to wail.

"You've woken Robert," she cried, rising to go to the baby.

"Sit down," he commanded. "I'll go and settle him. I'm quite intrigued to see how he looks since I saw him four days ago."

Karen watched nervously as he made his way to the bedroom. She was relieved when the baby stopped crying. *Perhaps he is holding him*, she thought, hoping that seeing the baby would calm him down.

In the bedroom, Alan gently rubbed the baby's downy cheek with his fingers. "Robert," he whispered. "Who are you?" He bit his lip as he felt his life was falling apart.

His phone rang. It showed his father's number. He gave the baby's cheek a pat. "Yes, dad?" he answered quickly.

"Glad you're back, Alan. Coming to the club? We can have a round of golf this afternoon."

#

Alan was pleased to see his father on the veranda of the club house as he drove the Volvo into the car park. He had always been close to his father, who had raised him by himself from when his mother died. There were nannies, of course, and, later, his father's second wife, but Alan always preferred to be with his father rather than his stepmother.

They greeted each other casually, there being no need for small talk between them. They began playing out of habit, Alan instantly relaxing as he felt the pleasure of the routine of the game.

"Good trip?" asked his father.

Alan took a shot and nodded. Finishing the first hole, they walked together.

"Karen all right? Everything happy at home?" his father asked suddenly.

Alan caught the tone of concern in his father's voice. "Yes. Why?" he said quickly.

"Her father tells me she thinks something might be wrong at work. She says you've been acting strangely."

"Me? She's the one. She's been a little odd since the baby was born. Seems too friendly with the caretaker. He's always hanging around on the penthouse floor. Dad, I'm worried. I don't think the baby's mine. He's very dark. Even his privates are nearly black."

They were at the third hole. "Ah, yes," his father said in a tone that made Alan pause in his stroke.

"Yes what, Dad?" Alan frowned.

"Well, son. You don't remember your mother, do you?"

"No, Dad, I was a year old when she died!"

"Of course. But you've seen her photos?"

"Sure. She was beautiful."

"Well, she was—"

"I know that," Alan said. "You told me she was American."

"She was. I met her in New Orleans when I was on a business trip. Actually, Alan, perhaps I should have told you this before.

She was certainly American. Afro-American to be exact. Born in New Orleans."

"You mean…?" Alan was speechless.

"Yes, your mother's mother, that means your grandmother, was of pure African descent. Her grandfather had been a slave in Louisiana, her parents were both black. She married a white man, though. He was a lawyer."

"So my mother was partly black?" He couldn't believe what he was hearing.

"Technically, yes. But she was very fair, Alan. She was even more beautiful than she looks in those old photographs. I loved her so much. All I have to remind me of her is you. You have her features, and her blood too."

He stared at his father in disbelief.

"So don't be suspicious of Karen, Alan. If your son looks a bit dark, it's because of you, a throwback to your mother's forefathers. It doesn't show in you because it can miss a generation. Be proud of your mother's blood, it's your inheritance from her."

Alan bit his lip until he tasted blood. His mother's blood… his blood… his son's. He smote the ball in anger. Both men watched in amazement as the ball soared into the sky, over the green, and dropped suddenly.

"Good gracious, Alan! I believe that's a hole in one! Congratulations."

"Thanks, Dad," he said, suddenly feeling happier than he had ever felt in his life before. At peace. "I've finished. Dad. I've got go home, to Karen… and to our son."

5. Low Tide

The sea sounded muffled when she woke that morning. She lay in the huge bed, her arm around a pillow, and listened, sleepily at first and then, as she concentrated on the thud of waves on the beach, more intently. She counted the seconds between each smack of the waves on the sand. One, two, three, five, ten. The sea was making a dull, dragging sound as the waves withdrew, paused as though to catch its breath, and then surged forward again. Usually the sea sounded angry; that morning it seemed as though its heart wasn't in it, as though it were weary of its routine but was making a token attempt to fulfil its natural function.

Puzzled, she switched on the bedside lamp. It was almost seven o'clock, time to get up. She unwound herself from the sheet and swung her feet out of bed, feeling the shock of the cold stone floor. One day, she thought, she would buy the bedside rug she had promised herself, but there always seemed to be more important things to buy, like food.

She wrapped the dressing gown around her, shivering slightly, although it wasn't really cold. She found her sandals and slipped them on. *Oh well*, she thought, *another day...* but she didn't feel inspired.

She listened again, straining to hear the waves. Since her husband died three years earlier, and she moved to the small beach house where they used to spend holidays (that he had left her in his will), she had lived alone. The sea's sound usually comforted her, reminding her that the sea washed other shores, thousands of miles away at the other side of the planet, where people lived other lives, had other loves. Today the sound was muted; there was no message in the air.

She recalled how a few days before, walking along the shore early in the morning, she had come across an empty wine bottle lying in the wet sand opposite her home. She swept it up eagerly. It had a cork and she could see a ball of paper inside.

She had carried the bottle with her to the beach house, found a corkscrew and opened it. She shook it vigorously until the ball of paper popped out. She had unrolled it slowly, wondering what pathetic message it would contain. Probably something from a child.

She spread the crumpled paper flat on the kitchen table and looked at the message. Three words: 'I love you.'

She had tossed the message, and the bottle, into the kitchen bin.

She walked, lost in thought, from the bedroom to the deck of the beach house. She was surprised to see a man was on the beach, gazing across the expanse of sand to the distant sea.

"Brett…" she called. "What's happened?"

The man turned, the early dawn light brightening the dusky hue of his craggy features. He was almost naked, wearing only a pair of old, faded denim jeans, frayed where he had cut them off to hang above his knees. The muscles of his chest rippled as he clenched and opened his fists.

She put her hand to her mouth to hide her gasp, as a surge of desire trickled through her.

"Low tide." The man shrugged as though it were of no importance and resumed gazing at the sea, seeming to dismiss her from his mind.

She longed to reach out over the wooden railing of the veranda deck and touch his bare, bronzed shoulders. She sighed to herself, wondering what to say, anything, to keep him there, to make him turn and face her so she could capture that image in her mind; the sun touching his cheeks so that he seemed to glow, as though he were part of the beach and the distant surge of the sea.

"You got up early," she said. "I didn't hear you go out."

"Low tide," he repeated. But his words were directed to the sea, and not to her. He bent and picked up a pebble, smooth as his skin and black as his eyes.

She watched, mesmerised, as he sent it skimming: three times, four, five... until it was devoured by the waves. He nodded, as though wishing the stone a safe journey, and then turned to face her. As his eyes bore into hers, she was shamefully aware that she was still clad in her sleeping attire, a stained, figure-hugging nightdress and her disreputable, almost transparent dressing gown.

"The stove needs lighting," he said. "I will see to it." He withdrew his gaze from her and made his way into the beach house from the side of the deck.

She stared after him. "Like a leopard," she thought. "He walks like a leopard."

The tide, knowing what it wanted to do, and with a mind of its own, gradually at first and then with wilder surges, swept over the shore. She watched, fascinated, as the efforts of a child's sandcastle were flattened in two sweeps of foam.

"Time to go," she told the sea. Pulling her dressing gown tightly to her body, she made her way inside.

The smell of coffee greeted her. And toast. Brett emerged from the galley, as he called the small kitchen. "Sit," he commanded. "Eat."

He had donned a T-shirt. Yellow and very dirty, it bore the faded image of a face and some unrecognisable lettering. *Probably foreign*, she decided.

Then, as always, and with no explanation, Brett nodded goodbye and walked out to the deck, down the steps to the beach and departed on his mysterious excursion, from which he would return at sundown.

Where does he go? she wondered.

Once she had followed him, keeping a great distance behind him, walking in his footprints along the beach. But he had turned and seen her. The look of anger on his face frightened her, and she retraced her steps back to the house. When he returned late that night, he didn't speak to her. He had brought a camp bed with him and set it up on the deck and slept there. Not for days did he acknowledge her. Never again would she follow him.

When the day had exhausted itself and darkness came, she curled, sleepless in the vast bed. She was aware that just a few feet from where she lay Brett would be stretched on the camp bed, still maintaining his puzzling aloofness. *Would he be asleep?* she wondered. *Would he be naked?*

She turned on her side, trying to ignore the temptation that was so near to her. She listened to the wind and the tide, watched the full moon mocking her through the curtainless window. "Who are you?" she whispered into the dark. "Who are you that I want you more than I ever did my husband?"

Brett had come into her life just six weeks before. He climbed on to the deck and knocked on the door, bobbing his head politely when she opened it. "Any odd jobs you want done, ma'am?"

She had stared at him in disbelief. Hs unruly dark hair

flopped over his brow and his eyes hinted at mischief. "I'm real, ma'am," he said with a grin. "From the village. Your gutter needs fixing."

That's not all, she thought, hoping he couldn't read her mind. "Oh, yes, it does."

"That's it then," he had said swinging his backpack off his shoulders and letting it fall to the deck. "I'm Brett." He held out his hand.

She took it eagerly thrilled by the squeeze of his fingers on her hand. "I'm... I'm Veronica."

He moved in that night.

#

She woke from her dreams, disturbed by a knock on the door. *Was it Brett?* No, he wouldn't knock. But it was after seven. She had slept too soundly and he would have gone already. Through the window she saw a tall girl, her long blonde hair billowing in the early morning breeze.

"Belinda!" she said, as she scrambled out of bed and opened the door, happy to see her young friend. "You're early. I was still asleep. No work today?"

"Photographer's sick," the girl said, lolloping into the house. She was so tall, she made everything in the room seem small.

Veronica made no comment, wondering why Belinda had become such a frequent visitor. She lived with her parents in the village but always seemed to be popping in, or hanging around on the beach outside the house. But she was careful not to come when Brett was around, as though she was watching to see when she was alone.

"Quiet today," Belinda said, her eyes roaming around the

61

room.

Veronica guessed she had seen the unmade bed through the open door to the bedroom. "Yes," she said. "Brett was here."

"Brett?" Belinda pursed her lips. "He's gone?"

Veronica nodded, not wanting to admit she didn't know what he was doing when he wasn't with her.

"Hmmm." Belinda threw herself down onto the settee, stretching out her long legs, her suntanned thighs protruding from her tight shorts. Those legs were her fortune, making her in demand as a fashion photographer's model. Veronica stepped around her carefully, not wanting to collide with Belinda's most important asset.

"Tea?"

Belinda shook her head. "I'm bored."

So that's why she's here." thought Veronica. "Surely you have a boyfriend?" she said aloud. "All those men you meet on photo shoots?"

Belinda seemed surprised. "Boyfriend? Me? Now why should I want a boyfriend?"

"Well," said Veronica. "With Brett, I sometimes wonder that myself."

Belinda stayed awhile, chatting about her career and the hopeless men she encountered on modelling shoots. "They all think I'm going to fall for them. Frankly I'm not interested."

When she stood up to go, she reached out to Veronica and hugged her, bending a little to give her quick kiss on her cheek. "I'm going for a walk on the beach," she said. "I like to do that early, when it's quiet. Just me and the sea."

Veronica watched her as she strode along the sand. The tide was coming in and Belinda, taking off her sandals, let the waves wash over her feet as she walked. Perhaps aware of Veronica's gaze, she turned and gave a cheery wave, shouting something that was drowned by the splash of the sea.

Veronica sighed. She padded into the bedroom and gazed at the tousled bed, the patchwork eiderdown fallen half onto the floor, and gave a rueful little laugh. "And I wonder," she said aloud, "what the beautiful Belinda would say if she knew the last time Brett and I shared this bed was over two weeks ago!"

She busied herself in making the bed respectable, stroking the pillow where once his head had lain, then headed to the galley to make herself a cup of coffee.

"What can I do to put things right between us?" she asked herself aloud. "And what on earth have I done to make him so unhappy with me? Why does he glare at me, and not meet my eyes?"

She put her hands over her ears to deaden the sound of the waves breaking on the shore, the sound which, for months after her husband had stormed out one night after a minor argument and simply disappeared, had mocked her and frightened her. It did still, even after a picnicking family had found him, rolling in and out with the tide. He had been dead for weeks. The waves had brought him home.

She shuddered. Taking a sip of coffee, she discovered she had slopped a few drops onto the tabletop, and had doodled a motif with her finger. It was a heart. "Oh Brett," she whispered to the empty room. "Why, when I turn to face you suddenly, are you looking at me with such passion? And why do you then turn away?"

Knowing that the chore of sweeping the floor of the small house, of shaking the mats, and of stock-taking the meagre contents of the pantry were beyond anything she could undertake in her present mood, she went out to the deck, ignoring his camp bed, but noting that his sleeping bag was tidily folded. And she gazed at the sea. *Will he come back tonight?* she wondered. *Or has he gone forever this time?*

He did come back in the evening, but was wrapped in his own thoughts, barely acknowledging the dinner she placed before him. He ate morosely, muttering occasionally as she tried to get him to talk, to say what it was that was troubling him. Again, he reminded her of a wild animal, self-possessed and impossible to tame.

After brooding over his half-empty plate for a while, he announced gruffly, "I'm going outside. I…" He stopped and looked at her. He shook his head. "It's nothing."

"Are you sure, Brett? Don't you want to tell me? What is it?" Even as she spoke, she knew she was saying the wrong thing.

"Nothing!" he said angrily. Then while she waited patiently, he said again, gently this time. "It's nothing. Go to sleep. I'll be outside."

The next day, she woke earlier than usual. She peered out of the window. Brett was still asleep on his camp bed, and she looked beyond him in the grey dawn to the beach. Someone was up already, walking along the sand at the tide's edge as it receded. She frowned.

"That's Belinda?" she said softly to herself.

Yes, it was. She was wearing a baggy top and jeans, disguising her beauty, but nevertheless there was no mistaking the lolloping way she moved. She seemed to be carrying something.

When she reached a spot opposite the house, she took a quick look around her and then knelt down and planted something in the sand, just beyond the tide's reach. She stood up, stretched, and continued her walk.

Veronica was intrigued. She opened the door to the deck and climbed down as quietly as she could, so as not to disturb the sleeping Brett. Quickly, although she was only wearing her night dress, she ran to see what Belinda had left.

It was an empty wine bottle, with a ball of paper inside. This bottle had a screw top, so Veronica opened it and shook out the ball of paper into her hand. She dropped the bottle back on the sand and began to unwrap the ball of paper. She was trembling.

There were three words on the paper written in pencil: 'I love you.'

Love who? thought Veronica. She turned back to the house. Brett was still stretched out on the camp bed. Suddenly, she was grasped from behind by two strong arms clamping her breasts, holding her firmly so she couldn't see who it was.

"You saw my message then?" It was Belinda's voice, whispering in her ears. "Now you know."

"Know what?" She managed to turn her head, only to meet Belinda's lips pressing on hers.

"Oh…" she spluttered, as she felt Belinda's tongue driving into her mouth. She wanted to struggle but couldn't, as a strange emotion soared through her. She felt herself surrendering to the warmth of Belinda's embrace. She glanced quickly over Belinda's shoulder at the house.

Brett was standing on the deck, watching. He turned abruptly, picked up his backpack and slung it over his shoulder, bent down and gathered the rolled-up camp bed under his arm, and stalked off the deck striding out along the sand. He didn't look back.

"Oh," said Veronica. "Where's he going?"

"Home to his wife, of course." Belinda took the stunned Veronica by her hand. "Oh dear," she said "You didn't know?' She paused, then said firmly "Come…"

She led Veronica across the beach, onto the deck and into the house.

6. The Artist

"I just loved this painting from the moment I saw it hanging on the park railings, so I bought it immediately," Mavis Biddle said, addressing thirty-three of her very close friends at her soiree; all ladies like her, of a certain age and unlimited wealth. "Of course, when I saw the artist the next day, I had to have him too."

The women twittered, while the tousled-haired youth standing self-consciously beside her, blushed.

"Isn't he cute?" Mavis tweaked the young artist's cheek. "And *so* talented, you've no idea! This boy is really going to be big, I assure you he is."

"He must be big already," said one of the women, bolder than the rest. "For you to be so interested."

Mavis shot her a look that would have killed her if her eyes had been a gun.

"May I remind you, *Miss* Delia Thorpe, that we are here to view my protégé's art, to give you and my *closest* friends, of whom I thought you were one, a chance to bid for his work before the price becomes absolutely astronomical."

Ryan Ryall, the young artist under appraisal by the women who thought themselves the city's trendsetters, bit his lip nervously. He had only agreed to this private exhibition at her town house as Mrs Mavis Biddle had promised him she would sell all his paintings and make him rich and famous. He had liked the idea when he met her the week before, as she descended from the limousine that drew up beside the park railings where he hung his paintings every day.

"You are the artist?" she had said, her voice trilling with excitement. "You look even better than the painting I bought yesterday, when you weren't here."

"I'm sorry," he said. "I was at home, painting. My friend told me someone in a limo had bought one of my works. I hope you haven't come to return it? I can't give a refund. I've spent the money on rent."

The woman had chuckled. "You have no idea, young man, what I can do, will do, for you. You have *such* talent." She reached over and ruffled his hair with long, thin fingers with nails, like talons, painted green.

"I am Mavis Biddle," she said in a husky voice. "I *make* artists famous… and rich. You have it, you know. I can tell."

Ryan nodded. He understood the glance she gave him, from head to toe and back up again. He was glad he was wearing his tight Levi's and not the baggy dungarees he wore when he was painting.

He knew he looked good. She wasn't the first person who was attracted by his bohemian nonchalance, well moulded cheek bones and blonde curls. He had learned through experience that his body and his art were his assets, and he had learned the power they gave him.

He studied the women gathered in the drawing room which had been converted with screens, on which he had hung his paintings, into a makeshift art gallery. He liked listening to Mavis Biddle praising his work. She was an expert, pointing out the subtleties in his composition, the creative use of brush strokes. He knew there would be a price to pay, not just her forty per cent commission, when the women bought his paintings.

"This is a silent auction," Mrs Biddle said slowly. "Just write your bid, minimum one thousand dollars, on the pad hanging beside each painting and sign it. There's champagne, it's Cristal 1996, from my husband's cellar, to help you decide."

Wow, that's before I was born, thought Ryan, pursing his lips. *I guess the commission's worth it.*

"I can assure you, Ryan has a beautiful body—" Mrs Biddle paused daring anyone to snigger, "—of work."

He bowed his head, his blond curls bouncing, as Mrs Biddle finished introducing his work, and the women clapped.

"There are only twenty paintings, so some of you will be disappointed. The highest bidder for each painting gets it," she said, when the applause died down. "Ryan will sign and date every painting you buy today which will add to their value."

"Will he add his phone number?" one of the women asked, to laughter from the others.

"Sure," said Ryan in a surprisingly mature voice coming from such an angelic, innocent face. "If you give me yours."

Mavis Biddle's smile tightened.

After half an hour of the women scurrying from painting to painting, writing on the pads, pausing only to take another glass of champagne from the butler, Mrs Biddle rang the silver hand bell she usually used to summon the butler.

"Ladies," she announced when she had their attention, "only ten minutes left. When I ring the bell again, the auction's closed."

Ryan watched in amazement at the flurry this announcement caused. As soon as one woman wrote down a bid on a pad beside a painting, another two descended and wrote their bids. He realised with a feeling of shame as well as exhilaration that some of the women never even looked at his paintings, only at how much the others were bidding.

"If all twenty paintings sell for a thousand dollars each," he thought with a flush of excitement, "I can paint without having to look for buyers in the park."

He sneaked a glance at Mrs Biddle. She was watching everyone very carefully, as though calculating how much each of her guests was bidding. Suddenly, she rang the bell vigorously.

"That's it," she said. "Julio will serve you more champagne while David, my accountant, will check the bids. Please have your cheque books ready. The winners must remove their paintings today."

Ryan declined an offer of champagne from the butler while Mrs Biddle conferred with David. She smiled with satisfaction as David tapped at his calculator and wrote a figure on a piece of paper and handed it to her.

Slowly, in pairs or groups, the friends of Mrs Mavis Biddle bade farewell to their host, who stood with her hand upon the shoulder of Ryan Ryall, as though he were a piece of lost property she had just reclaimed. Ryan, enjoying himself immensely, treated each retreating lady with a special look, which flamed their faces and played havoc to the area around their knicker elastic.

After the ladies had left, followed by their drivers carrying the paintings they had bought, Mrs Biddle sat down and beckoned Ryan to sit beside her. "I was right," she said. "They love you and," she added hastily, "your art."

"How much did the paintings sell for?" he asked, hoping it was more than the five hundred dollars he would have got for each painting by selling them off the park railings.

"Eighty-six thousand dollars," she said, waving the slip of paper under his nose. "So less my forty per cent commission and the cost of the two cases champagne, about—"

"Champagne?" he said in shock. "Doesn't that come out of your commission?"

"No, sweetie pie." She kissed him on his cheek before he could move away.

"So when do I get the money then?" he asked bluntly, without his usual charming smile. "Today?"

"No, Ryan, poppet. I'll phone you when the cheques have cleared. I don't trust some of those women at all."

Ryan looked at her, as though seeing Mavis Biddle for the first time. He stood up as it occurred to him only then that perhaps she wasn't to be trusted either.

#

Mrs Tabitha Winstanley and Miss Delia Thorpe sat at their favourite table in the Palm Restaurant, partaking of afternoon tea and awaiting the arrival of Constance and Barbara. Antoine, the restaurant's owner, who was especially proud of his afternoon tea arrangement for ladies of a certain age and blue hair rinses, hovered near the table.

He was worried about the multi-tiered cake stand. One rather large lady had already sampled so many tit-bits that the whole affair looked rather pathetic. He hoped that the other two ladies would arrive soon. His smile was beginning to hurt, and so were his feet. He retreated for a few moments to the kitchen, leaving the ladies to themselves.

Delia, chasing a cream slice over her plate and losing the race, turned to Tabitha and asked, "Are you a virgin, dear?"

At that moment Tabitha had been in the process of endeavouring to cut a meringue the size of a miniature Taj Mahal into bite-size pieces with a fork. She spluttered, and sent a shower of sugared crumbs over the table, and adorned her face with cream and the neck-line of her blouse with the efforts of the pastry cook.

"Of course I'm not a..." (she paused to look over her shoulder, but Antoine was not around)—virgin?" she said in surprise. "I've got two strapping sons and umpteen grandchildren."

"But," asked the unmarried Delia, "have you been a virgin since you were widowed?"

Tabitha was saved from answering by the arrival of the two expected friends. Mrs Constance Van Crighton and the Honourable Barbara Beecham.

"Bloody hell!" exclaimed Barbara, manoeuvring her massive backside onto the dainty chair which had been saved for her by Delia and Tabitha. "That bloody woman! Mavis Bloody Biddle! God, I hate her with aspirations to be a trendsetter, just because her husband's wealthy. The bitch! And that poor little sod she's got her claws into, the artist chappie. God help him." She reached over and grabbed an oozing eclair.

Constance, who had married her husband for love, not money, and was disappointed in the former, remarked, "But I wouldn't mind a brush-stroke from that cute Ryan Ryall. Wouldn't you?" They all agreed, except for The Hon. Barbara, who was out-of-the-closet gay, as well as being an unabashed Brit.

#

Ryan was puzzled. He sat in the subway and wondered what had happened. Mavis Biddle, having declared herself tired after the afternoon spent persuading thirty-three ladies to compete for his

71

paintings, had retired to her bedroom. He had to borrow five dollars from David to get home. And yet those twenty paintings had earned him more than forty thousand dollars, even after her commission. He was rich—or was he?

Mavis Biddle had promised all sorts of things that would make him famous. She had said she would arrange for him to attend film premiers escorting up-and-coming film stars where he would be photographed, he would be her guest at all the events on society's calendar, she would get an article about him in *Vogue*.

"We must make people talk about you," she had said.

The next morning, having nothing else to do, he gathered up a few of his paintings that he still had in his loft studio and, with a friend to drive him, went back to the park and hung his paintings on the railings. He did that every day for a week. Nobody bought a single one and Mavis Biddle didn't phone. His cash was running out, the rent on the studio was due.

The weather changed. The sun of the summer that brought people to the park abruptly turned to rain. Ryan decided he could wait no longer. He phoned Mrs Biddle.

It was David who answered. "She's gone away," he said. "I don't know when she'll be back."

"What about my money? Have the cheques cleared."

"Ooooh…" David paused. "Didn't Madam tell you?"

"Tell me what?"

"She asked me to put the money in an account for you. Don't worry about the five dollars you owe me. I took that out first."

"What account? How can I get my money?"

There was silence then David said slowly, "Do you have anything in writing? A written agreement with Madam, I mean."

Ryan had the feeling that life was not only catching up with him, but overtaking him on the inside lane. If he made the wrong move, he would crash.

"Of course I have," he said quickly, hoping David wouldn't know he was lying. He hadn't even slept with Mavis Biddle, although that seemed to be what she wanted. He needed to make sure she fulfilled her promises. That was his only bargaining ploy.

"I'll phone you when she returns," said David, cutting off the call.

Ryan stared at the silent phone unhappily. Then, as he was about to return it to his pocket, he remembered the woman at the soiree who had pressed her business card into his hand.

"I'm a lawyer," she had said with a British accent. "Let me know if you need any help." She had flashed a glance in Mavis Biddle's direction and then passed on to view the paintings. He had noticed that she was the only woman who didn't bid on anything, although she studied each of his paintings carefully and seemed to like his work. None of the others, who actually bid, paid so much attention to each painting.

"I've been expecting your call," the Hon Barbara Beecham said when he phoned her that afternoon.

#

Ryan gazed around his studio in the loft of the old apartment building, hoping he had made it look a bit less squalid. He had swept the wooden boards of the floor, flicked a duster around and cleared the sink of unwashed plates. The empty cheap wine bottles he hastily banished to the bottom of the wardrobe to be dealt with later. He was expecting a visitor.

Looking at himself in a mirror, he decided he needed to

smarten up. He rummaged through the few clothes in the closet and was relieved to find a clean smock top, which would safely cover his paint-stained jeans. He brushed his golden curly hair until it hung down over his ears in shiny ringlets.

He laughed to himself. "I don't think the British lady will be one bit interested in how I look."

He realised he was nervous. He had never met an 'Hon' before, especially a bossy, butch one. Frankly, he had found the Hon. Barbara, a British viscount's daughter, rather terrifying when they had been introduced at the soiree. She had regarded him through a monocle, silent but smiling slightly. He had felt extremely uncomfortable. Yet she was the only woman who had given him her card, and yesterday he had phoned her in desperation.

The meeting had been arranged for midday, and it was now one-thirty. He had suggested on the phone that they meet in the park, but Barbara had insisted on coming to the studio.

She arrived at two o'clock. Humming under her breath, she surveyed the small attic studio before stopping to study each of the paintings that were propped up along the walls, peering at them intently through her monocle. Then she extracted a heavy magnifying glass from her Gucci shoulder bag and inspected each one minutely.

Ryan found her behaviour odd and extremely unsettling. "They're not copies," he said with a hint of anger. "And I don't paint by numbers and I haven't stolen them! I just want your advice on how to get the forty thousand dollars your friend Mavis Biddle owes me!"

The Honourable Barbara Beecham treated him to a slow smile and replied, "No Ryan, I can see they're not forgeries, or copies or stolen. They're all brilliant. But just you tell me exactly who you are and where you learned to paint like an urban Gaugin." And she patted the seedy couch on which she had perched herself, and bade him to "Sit!"

#

Delia, Tabitha, Constance and the Hon. Barbara sat in sticky contentment around the table at the Palm Restaurant, whilst Antoine looked in horror at the relic of the cake stand. Nothing left, just crumbs. Bowing to the ladies, and with his smile slipping he returned to his kitchen to revive himself with a nip of cognac.

"Well," exclaimed Mrs Tabitha Winstanley, secretly loosening the zipper on her skirt, "and where do we all think Mavis Biddle has taken herself off to?"

"Gotten herself another protégé," retorted Constance, who read romantic novels, and was now removing a cluster of crumbs from her ample neck line.

"Oh my word," twittered Delia Thorpe, shaking pieces of jam sponge from her lap, "do you think she has kidnapped Ryan and made him her slave?"

Barbara, the Honourable, just smiled and, brushing crumbs of strudel from her waistcoat and tie, said, in her best London Belgravia voice, "We'll all hear lots more about that young man, don't you worry."

The ladies, in unison, turned their faces towards Barbara, awaiting the snippet of gossip that seemed to be forthcoming, but were disappointed as the Honourable just tapped the side of her nose and winked. "You'll see," she said, "all in good time."

"Honestly, Barbara," grumbled Tabitha, "if you know anything about the whereabouts of Mavis and the gorgeous Ryan,

I really think you should share the secret with us! After all, except for you, we all purchased his paintings."

"Do you think she's set up a love nest for herself and Ryan, and become his nude model?" asked the romantically inclined Delia.

"If so, he'll need an exceptionally thick brush," retorted Constance.

As no cakes or pastries remained on the three-tiered stand, the quartet prepared to leave, after squabbling and niggling over how much money each owed as their share of the bill. Then, scrabbling about under the table for the four pairs of shoes that had been slipped off under cover of the formerly spotlessly white damask tablecloth and collecting their handbags, the ladies, full of cake and puffing slightly, made their way to the hairdressing salon, which was their next port of call.

The Hon. Barbara, however, had work to do. She instructed her driver to take her to the park where Ryan hung his paintings. When she arrived, her bosom pal, with the accent on bosom, Roxanne Le Tissier, was already there. She was ignoring an anxious-looking Ryan as she studied each of the paintings with the same scrupulous intensity Barbara herself had shown.

Ryan saw the limousine arriving and ran to the edge of the sidewalk to open the door. "Oh, Miss Beecham," he said in surprise. "Welcome. I thought it was Mrs Biddle."

"Yes," said Barbara with a throaty chuckle. "We use the same limo service." She turned away from him. "What do you think, Roxanne?"

"You know each other?" Ryan asked in surprise.

"Of course," said Barbara. "Roxanne is my partner. She owns Le Tissier Gallery."

Ryan stared at two women as they greeted each other with a

fulsome kiss on the lips. Le Tissier Gallery was the city's most prestigious art gallery. Only the world's top painters were ever invited to exhibit there. Suddenly, Ryan felt nervous.

"What do I think?" said Roxanne. "Ryan, is all this your own work?"

Before he could answer, Barbara spoke for him. "Yes, it is. I went to his studio and he showed me where and how he works."

"Let me hear it from him."

"Yes, madam," he said releasing his most charming smile.

"I see you only have cityscapes," Roxanne said. "Bold and beautiful, alive and intricate they are. Superb in detail and characterisation, they have a great impact but, but, but…"

"Boring!" interrupted Barbara. The two women had been together for so long, she knew her partner's mind. It was her own opinion too.

"I paint what I see," said Ryan, upset by the criticism.

"What you see from your attic studio window?"

"Why, yes." He was about to add, "How do you know?" but Barbara raised a large hand to stop him.

"Could you paint something else?" Roxanne looked around the park. "Nature, for instance?"

Ryan felt offended. "Of course," he said. "Anything, but not commissioned portraits. I see people as they are from their souls. They don't like it when their portraits turn out to be ugly."

"He's got it!" Roxanne said to Barbara. "You are right."

"As always," Barbara said with a knowing smile.

"What's this all about?" Ryan felt uncomfortable being discussed as though he wasn't there. "Did you get my money from the Biddle woman?"

"Oh yes," she said, pulling an envelope out of her large shoulder bag. "Here's the cheque. Eighty-six thousand dollars in full, no commission, or champagne charged."

"How…?"

"We lawyers have a way, you know, young man. David caved in as soon as I mentioned what I know about him."

Ryan looked at the cheque and shook his head in disbelief.

"It's a good thing you never signed anything with Mrs Biddle. She won't bother you again."

Ryan sighed. "She said she'd make me famous…"

"Your art will do that," said Roxanne. "You don't have to sell your body as well."

"What…?" Ryan was shocked. "I didn't…"

"That's all right. Nothing to do with me. It's your future as a painter that I'm investing in." Roxanne looked around the sidewalk. "You need to broaden your vision," she said. "We need variety. Get away from cityscapes. Paint escapism."

"But I live here. This cheque will keep me going for a year while I paint."

Barbara put her hand heavily on Ryan's shoulder. "No, Ryan. Roxanne and I want you to go away. To Tahiti, to add colour and escapism to your art. It worked for Gaugin."

"Come to my gallery tomorrow," said Roxanne, "and we'll organise everything."

"You'll see. You'll be famous." Barbara patted him on his back in a fatherly way.

"We are going to sponsor you to go to Tahiti," said Roxanne. "And when you return you shall have your first real exhibition in Le Tissier Gallery. Your paintings will sell for at least fifty thousand dollars *each*."

Ryan nodded his head slowly, brushed back his curls from his face and grinned mischievously. "Can I have that in writing?"

7. Mr Frobisher's Hobby

Mr Frobisher lay in bed, following strict instructions from his wife not to move. She herself had risen a good twenty minutes earlier than usual, and was in one of her annoyingly girlish and twittering moods. She had opened the curtains, and the early sun was mocking and almost blinding him as he screwed up his eyes against the blaze. His bladder was full, but he knew how very hurt and upset his wife would be should she come into the bedroom and find he was in the lavatory.

Busy sounds of kitchen activity reached his ears, and soon came the smell of bacon. Mr. Frobisher's worst fears were founded. He was to have breakfast in bed. It was his birthday.

Birthdays, as a whole, were fairly bearable. Usually, a nice steak dinner and a glass or two of red wine, and a trifle. But since Mr Frobisher had retired five years previously, his wife had insisted on buying him *hobbies*. He had endured her silly, insufferable gifts for four birthdays. And today, he would be introduced to her next whim for himself. Over the years, since he had become a pensioner, his presents included a fishing rod with reel; bait box and folding stool; a beer making kit; a potter's wheel and the lamentable tricycle! These hobbies now cluttered the garden shed, waiting for him to 'get around to them'.

Mrs Frobisher kicked the bedroom door open with her foot, and balancing the loaded tray in the crook of her arm, closed it with a shove of her bottom. "Happy Birthday, dear," she twittered. "Did you think I'd forgotten?"

"No such luck," he muttered to himself.

"I've got a little something for you, dear," she continued. "Shut your eyes whilst I heave it in."

"Heave it in?" He panicked. Whatever had she got him? A horse?

She disappeared for a moment, then returned, holding a large, square box. *Not a horse, then.* "Open it, dear," she commanded. "It's a hobby for you."

"Oh God," he thought, fumbling with the string. And there on the bed lay the new 'hobby' she had bought for him. Binoculars.

"Try them on, dear," she trilled.

How on earth," he wondered, *"did one 'try on' binoculars?*

Of course, the strap went round his neck.

"Oh, you *do* look handsome," she simpered, "in your striped jim-jams and slung binoculars. Just like an explorer!"

But there was something else in the box.

"A camera," exclaimed his wife, her voice rising a decibel, as it usually did when she was excited. "You attach it to the binoculars, and 'zoom, click and print,' it says on the box."

Mr Frobisher was appalled! He stared at the alien apparatus. It looked terrifying. He then realised that the lower lip of his wife was beginning to tremble, and she was sniffing, so he quickly said, "Thank you, dear. It's exactly what I wanted."

"You must take a photograph right now, to celebrate your birthday," she demanded, removing the breakfast tray from his lap and leaving him with a slice of toast in his hand and taking the yellow yolk of egg on his plate which he had been saving to eat last.

"But my dear," he said, "I have yet to discover how it all

works." He gazed at the pile of paraphernalia spread out on the duvet. "There seems to be an awful lot of gadgets."

"Read the instructions, dear," his wife said as though talking to a child. "Oh," she continued, her eyes glazing with far-away dreams, "this new hobby could be the making of you. You could become a famous photographer, like Lord Snowdon."

Mr Frobisher kept silent although he wanted to say 'I really don't think so, dear,' but that would cause a fuss on his birthday.

#

The Frobishers had been married for fifty years; in fact, it had been their Golden Wedding anniversary the previous April. They had celebrated quietly and without fuss. A few cards and bouquets from distant relatives, and a pair of gold earrings and pearl cufflinks shyly left by the breakfast plates from and to each other.

There were no children from the marriage, for the simple reason that Mr Frobisher never got the hang of things in that department, and Mrs Frobisher didn't want him to. On the very rare occasions they had tried it, Mr Frobisher had wondered if the operation had been completed and it if was all right for him to stop, whilst Mrs Frobisher had spent the time planning the following week's menus. But the marriage was a contented and happy one.

Sometimes, though, Mr Frobisher wished his spouse wasn't quite so 'wifey'. In fact, at the moment, he was in quite a bad mood. It had taken him simply hours to erect the camera on the screw-in tripod and fix it to the binoculars and the small portable printer, and just as he thought he had nailed it, the silly contraption had come apart in his hands and he had to start all over again.

The instruction manual was extremely unhelpful, and to cap it all, Mrs Frobisher insisted on calling out to him, asking if he had 'snapped anything exciting'. He decided to make the guest bedroom his photographic studio, since they never had any guests and they had another spare bedroom as well. Removing the mirror from the dressing table he had an admirable bench for his paraphernalia, and at last thought he could possibly be ready to 'zoom, click, save and print.'

He would practise, he decided, by taking a photo from the open window. But the view from the guest bedroom was rather disappointing. A corner of the shed, the wheelbarrow full of weeds on the patio, and a bit of apple tree. But oh, what luck. There was his neighbour, Mrs Swindley, bringing her washing in. He had a very good view of her if he turned slightly sideways. And she had such a pretty yellow dress on, which blended well with the sky.

Mr Frobisher aimed his camera, tried to remember where all the different buttons and knobs were, shut his eyes and 'zoomed and pressed'. Seconds later, to his astonishment and delight, a perfect photograph spewed itself from a little slot at the side of the camera onto his work bench. But—oh my goodness! Mrs Swindley must have bent down to place a piece of laundry in her wash basket, because Mr Frobisher was holding in his hand a picture of a very ample and comely bottom, encased in blue satin. Greatly enlarged.

He was horrified. But then, he experienced a strange feeling in his loins, the likes of which had never occurred before, and instead of tearing the offending photograph into tiny pieces and flushing them down the lavatory, he tucked it into his wallet, in the very secret compartment behind the press stud. And, to calm his bewilderment and appease his wife, he quickly zoomed and snapped a blackbird on the corner of the shed. Mrs Frobisher was delighted and said she would have it framed.

That night in bed, Mr Frobisher surprised his wife.

#

The next morning, Mrs Frobisher was pleased when her husband asked her to pack him a picnic, as he wanted to spend a day 'getting to know' his new hobby. (He had secretly named the combined apparatus as his 'Binicam').

Off he set, with a spring in his step and a breast of cold chicken, salad and crusty bread in his knapsack. Around his neck swung his Binicam, bouncing against his waistcoat buttons. He wore the look of an artist surveying the surroundings for suitable composition. He even narrowed his eyes and shook his head and raised and lowered his binoculars in exasperation, as he awaited something apt, something 'zoomable'.

As he made his way along the narrow path beside the river, he tripped, nearly falling over. He looked crossly at what had nearly caused his accident, and discovered it was a lady's shoe. A few paces along, his feet became entangled in a pair of lacy knickers, of minute proportions. Kicking them off his shoe he heard the sound of gentle snoring, coming from a clump of tall reeds by the side of the path.

Stealthily, Mr Frobisher edged his way forward, parted the thick grass, and there—oh my goodness, his heart gave such a leap—there was the woman who ran the mobile library, stark naked, having a nude nap!

With a shaking hand, the Binicam recorded the scene with a little flash and a pop, and a slither of wonderful photography fell onto the path. As he later limped his way back home, after placing the naughty photograph alongside the one of his neighbour's bottom in his wallet, he remembered just in time to take a snap of a duck on the river. Mrs Frobisher was over the moon with it.

That night, after another surprise, Mrs Frobisher decided she would wear her tights in bed in future.

\#

The following day was a bit of a disappointment to Mr Frobisher. In fact, the shocking event caused him to have one of his funny turns, which his wife put down to too much sun and not wearing protective headgear.

He had decided to wander the woods, to see what was what. He had heard a sound, and, creeping stealthily towards it (*Like a Red Indian*, he thought) he was shocked beyond belief to come upon Mr Bullard, the Scout Master, standing facing a tree and… oh my goodness… what on earth was he doing? The disgusting man! No wonder his spectacles had very thick lenses!

Mr Frobisher crept away, like an Indian in retreat, but not before he had yet another photograph to add to his collection. Trudging home, sick at heart and with his picnic uneaten, Mr Frobisher experienced a new sensation descend upon him. It didn't interfere with his loins this time, but he suddenly felt all-powerful, a man with the know-all and see-all and wherewithal! He felt ten feet tall!

Mrs Frobisher took herself to the spare room to sleep.

\#

Mr Frobisher had taken to wearing a red cravat, navy blue beret and his lightweight cream blazer. His wife was delighted and proud to see how the new hobby she had created for her husband was working out, and she now had a wonderful array of his photographic efforts awaiting to be framed. They were mostly of ducks and birds and river and bits of trees, but they were, to her, beautiful.

She was a bit concerned about the strange attire he had started to wear; it was as though she was married to a man to whom she hadn't properly been introduced. More worrying was the bedroom activity. She hoped that it was a passing phase and that he would soon grow out of it.

But Mr Frobisher was taking his new career very seriously indeed. Today, for instance, he had decided to pay another visit to the river, because the past few days had been a bit of a disappointment, and 'zoom, click, print' had only brought forth evidence that the owner of the local restaurant was, as all suspected, poaching trout from the private part of the river, right where the notice said 'No Fishing.'

Down a side alley, looking through a tiny window at the back of the post office, he was surprised to see the Post Mistress steaming open some envelopes before they were due for delivery. But as luck would have it, as she leant forward to read the latest gossip, she inadvertently showed almost all of her left bosom, including a glimpse of dark brown nipple! One more photo to add to his collection.

Mr Frobisher decided to try his luck in the woods again, and, as he crept between the trees, he encountered the vicar's Lambretta scooter and a lady's bicycle hidden in the bushes. Then he heard the sound of combined grunts and squeals. And there before him a naked bottom was raised... and lowered... and raised... and, trying to keep the Binicam steady, on the upward view of the backside, he could see a tattooed anchor.

There was also writing, and Mr Frobisher, waiting for a few ups and downs, managed to read through the binoculars 'Up Anchor.' It took a good half dozen zooms and clicks to record the procedure. Then Mr Frobisher made his way home, with aching loins, wondering who on earth had been on the receiving end of that tattooed bottom.

Mrs Frobisher locked herself into the spare bedroom and put a chair under the handle.

#

The next morning Mr Frobisher woke with a sense of foreboding and gloom. He knew the feeling well, it happened every year, usually not long after he received his birthday present. He admitted to himself that he was bored with his new hobby.

He would have to tell his wife. But during breakfast a jolly good plan began to form in his mind, and, dressed in his artistic attire, he strode out on what he hoped to be his last outing with Binicam.

There was a little rustic bridge spanning the river a few miles from where he set out, and, standing in the very middle, facing east and looking furtively around to make sure he was alone, he unhooked the apparatus from around his neck and dropped it into the river. At first it seemed to put up a fight, but then with a sad little popping noise, it slowly sank out of sight. Mr Frobisher was extremely relieved and hastened home to tell his wife a little white lie.

Mrs Frobisher was very upset to hear of the loss of the binocular/camera with attached printer. But as she kept telling her husband, it could have been much, much worse. It could have been *he* who had fallen into the river when that cow had bellowed so closely and startled him into dropping his lovely birthday present and putting an end to his hobby.

So, it seemed that everything had turned out all right—apart from those dratted photographs. The only sensible thing to do, Mr Frobisher told himself, was to borrow his wife's dressmaking scissors, cut the damned things into shreds and flush them away. But there still remained in his mind a little wisp of final naughtiness.

He arose from his bed at two the next morning, and dressed hurriedly in warm clothes. He could hear Mrs Frobisher snoring in the spare room. Silently he made his way downstairs and out into the cold night air. A full moon lit his way as he clutched the bundle of incriminating photographs in his gloved hand.

Firstly, he posted the one of his neighbour's wonderful knickered bottom through her letterbox. Then a short walk to the bungalow where the mobile library lady lived. The image of her beautiful naked body plopped through the mailbox onto the mat inside her door.

With much distaste, the photograph of Mr Bullard pleasuring himself, Mr Frobisher placed under the empty milk bottle on the step of the scout master's cottage. "And I don't care if the milkman sees it," he said to himself.

It was quite a long walk to his next port of call, the restaurant where the poaching owner lived with his wife and family in the upper storey. There was a proper mailbox by the door, a good, solid wooden structure, and Mr Frobisher dropped the photo he had had taken inside.

He had been rather clever with his arrangements for the delivery of the picture depicting the bosom of the Post Mistress. He had placed it in an envelope and addressed it to her, putting on a 2nd class stamp. This he posted in the public letter box outside the Post Office, where the addressee herself would find it.

This left the one photograph that was a bit of a worry. Who on earth was under that tattooed posterior? There seemed to be just the one option open to Mr Frobisher, so he posted it through the letter box of the vicar. And then he returned home to bed.

#

For a few weeks the village had a discontented, rather furtive air about it. People who met in the street would politely nod, but not stop to chat. The vicar kept his sermons short. But after a while, things improved, and the recipients of those dreadful photographs began to relax as the dread of any forthcoming blackmail communication abated.

Mrs Swindley made sure she always wore slacks when she hung out her washing. The mobile library lady said, "Sod it," and continued to sunbathe in the nude by the river.

The local restaurateur continued to poach for trout, but found himself a much better and more secluded spot. Mr Bullard, greatly upset, took his own personal fetish further into the woods. The postmistress still steamed open various envelopes, but did so in her bedroom, and took to wearing high-necked sweaters.

As for the vicar... "Darling," said his wife, who was more forgiving than he was, "When the sap is rising and you feel like a little bit of open-air nooky, don't you think we should find somewhere not so near home?"

#

Mrs Frobisher moved back into the marital bedroom, and she and her husband resumed their marital position, which was back-to-back with a bit more pressure in the winter months

Meanwhile, Mr Frobisher secretly wallowed in his newly-discovered self-confidence. He had found himself a new hobby. He joined his local Amateur Dramatic group and attended the preliminary read through of the script. To his joy, he secured a part in the forthcoming Christmas production of *Dick Whittington*. Mr Frobisher was cast as King Rat. He had yet to break the news to his wife.

8. The Eye of the Beholder

Mo was annoyed to find her usual seat on the beach promenade had been taken by a kissing couple. This was her preferred seat, one which could have been specially placed for her. It stood slightly back from the other line of benches, half hidden in the trees but still with a good view of the beach and sea.

Mo had almost decided to return back home to eat her picnic lunch, but noticed at the opposite end of the prom another bench, tucked away in the shade of a tree. As two overflowing rubbish bins spewed their contents around the surrounding area, she supposed it was not a popular choice for anyone to sit.

Taking a deep breath and tying her headscarf tighter under her chin, she made her way along the prom to the seat. With her eyes cast down and head bowed low, she was still fully aware of the gasps and whispering of people, in pairs, groups or alone, as she passed by. A child with a dog-on-wheels toy stared and pointed, and his mother drew him closer to her. Mo pulled the scarf more firmly, trying to disguise as best she could her birthmarked face.

At last, she sat, in seclusion and away from the horrified or ghoulish stares. She unwrapped her sandwiches. Alarmed, she saw a gentleman heading straight to the seat on which she had settled. He was very dapper, very smart in his blue blazer and cream trousers. He approached, nearer and nearer, until he was just a few feet away from her.

"Oh," she said, "I'm so sorry. Is this where you usually sit? I'm normally at the other end of the prom, but someone has pinched my bench."

The man halted, and seemed shocked. Then he chuckled. "Oh, that's all right, my dear," he said. "I don't mind sharing with a nice young lady. Just shuffle yourself along a bit, and as a true gent I will take the smelly bin end."

By habit she adjusted her head scarf until it resembled a yashmak. "*Nice young lady*?" she thought. Nobody in the whole of her life had called her that! He was all right, she decided, and she felt safe.

He started talking about the seagulls, telling her which squawks belonged to which species. He remarked upon the wonderful scent of the wild mint that grew in clusters behind their bench. He pointed out how to tell the call of a swift from that of a swallow.

Mo unwrapped her lunch. Shyly she asked, "Would you like a sandwich? They're only cheese, I'm afraid."

"My favourite," the man beamed, helping himself. The clock above the pavilion struck one, and the gentleman stirred himself. "My turn to bring the picnic tomorrow," he said, rising. "Oh," he continued, turning to her, "you *will* be here tomorrow, won't you?"

"I'll be here," she promised.

He smiled, and slowly walked away.

She watched him until he was out of sight. "*He must be double my age*," she thought. "*He must be in his sixties. But*," she marvelled, "*he talked to me!*"

The next day, Mo had lost all confidence in hoping that her new friend would turn up for their lunch time meeting. He had promised to bring a picnic for them, but Mo deliberated on whether to make a round of sandwiches for herself in case he didn't show. She decided not to. She found herself hoping against hope that he would keep their date. *Is this a date?* she asked herself. If so, it would be her first one ever!

She busied herself in getting ready. She brushed her rather beautiful, naturally wavy chestnut hair over the top half of her birthmark, and tied the scarf, which was so much part of her that it was like a second skin, over her head and under her chin. She unplugged her sewing machine, fed her cat, and then made her way to the park.

She sat on 'their' bench, shaking and nearly crying. She had walked past her usual, well-loved seat and it had been vacant. She hovered a moment, wondering if she would be brave enough to walk to the other end of the prom, past all those people, and see if her gentleman friend showed up. She was heckled and scorned by a drunken man, who called out terrible things, and waved his bottle of cider at her.

She sighed. Her new friend wasn't there, but she hadn't expected him to be. Then, after a few moments, he came walking towards the seat, and she stood up and called out, "Oh, you came."

He sat beside her. "There you are, m'dear," he said happily, as he spread a beautifully white handkerchief on the bench before he sat. "I've been thinking about you all night. I was dreading you not being here."

Mo was silent. Not having been in this position before she supposed she was being 'chatted up.'

"I've brought our picnic as promised," he said. "Ham rolls and a couple of nice apples."

They sat and ate, whilst he quizzed her on which bird sounds she had memorised from their meeting the day before. Suddenly he asked "What is your name? I can't keep calling you 'm'dear'."

"Well," she replied, "It's Mo."

"*Mo!*" he exclaimed, "What sort of damn fool name is that?"

She answered shyly, "My real name is Maureen, but it gets shortened to Mo."

"But Maureen is a splendid name," he said. "And what's more, *my* name is Maurice, so we almost match."

"Mo and Maurice," she giggled. "We sound like the name of a bespoke tailors." She realised that this was the first time she had ever cracked a joke.

Maurice laughed uproariously. "I shall call you Maureen from now on," he promised.

The pavilion clock struck one, far too soon. They arranged to meet the next day. She planned to make a quiche.

Their third meeting proved to be a 'getting to know you' morning. Maurice discovered that Maureen worked from home, making dresses for little girls on a commission basis for a store in Soho.

To her delight, Maurice composed music for the piano. He had, he told her, a small electronic keyboard at home. He admitted that he had once been married, albeit for a very short time, and had no children. He asked Maureen if she was married, divorced, or 'spoken for'.

"None of those three, Maurice," she replied.

On the Sunday, Maureen knew that she might as well stay in and have a Ready Meal For One. Apparently, on Sundays Maurice played the organ for his local church, and Maureen didn't go to church. But on Monday he was there on the bench even before she arrived. It was his turn for the picnic, and it was a good'un. Pork pies and hard-boiled eggs. And a punnet of strawberries.

As they munched, they were aware of distant music, a sort of 'thump, thump, thump'. "The band stand," exclaimed Maurice, excitedly. "They've got a band!"

Arm-in-arm they made their way to the lines of deckchairs erected in a circle and listened, enthralled to a slightly out-of-practice group of uniformed men playing old tunes that Maurice sang along to. And then that blasted clock chimed one, and they said goodbye.

The next day, Tuesday, sitting on their special park bench, Maurice kissed her. The first kiss from *anybody* that she had ever received in her life. He just turned to face her, put his hand under her chin, and gently kissed her on the lips.

Then he slowly eased the headscarf to the back of her head and stroked that wonderful, thick hair. His fingers traced the outline of the angry, raised birthmark which covered the left side of her face.

"Shall we go and get a cup of tea from the kiosk?" he asked. "That is, if it's open."

"Oh," said the flustered Maureen, "it's open. I passed it on my way here."

"Right," said Maurice, standing up. "Tea it is! And I tell you what, we'll jolly well stay out *all* afternoon." But then he sat down again, and pulled Maureen to him.

"Tell you what, Maureen," he said quietly. "Isn't it about time you took that silly scarf off! I think you are the most beautiful woman in the world, and sod what the rest of them think! I am so proud to be with you."

And he gently untied her scarf and placed it on top of the rubbish bin beside him. She smiled and kissed him.

Together they made their way, hand-in-hand to the tea kiosk. They gently swung their arms in rhythm to the music from the band stand. Slowly they merged into the landscape of other people, other lives.

Maureen and Maurice walked together, in their new-found love. She with her disfigurement, and he with his white cane.

9. On Business

The purser crossed herself as the plane began its run up for take-off. Gus was sitting in 1E, the port side aisle seat in First Class, from where he could see into the galley where the cabin crew were seated. The purser sat with her back to the cockpit, facing the passengers, strapped into her seat with a harness, not a simple seat belt like everyone else. She was a petite woman, neatly dressed in a formal black outfit.

Gus hoped her appeal to God would be sufficient to get them airborne. He had no fear of flying, unlike the purser, only a fear of flying uncomfortably. If the plane had First Class, he wanted to be sitting in it. He recognised there was probably a psychological reason for that but for him, flying should be done in comfort. He didn't mind staying in the cheapest accommodation on land, but when he was spending hours sitting in a tube hurtling through the sky at 30,000 feet above sea level, he wanted the best.

As a sixty-five-year-old widower still practising as an architect, living alone in an apartment in Dubai, with children in England in good jobs, he could afford it. His wife, who had died ten years before and whom he never missed, had nagged him constantly about spending too much money during their thirty years of unhappy marriage.

When he was travelling as a backpacking hippy in Economy Class, he used to pour scorn on the poor rich slobs who spent so much money to fly First Class. However, that was in the 1970s when flying was fun, even in Economy.

He recalled once, flying from Istanbul to Amsterdam, how he had bought a dozen oysters in their shells on the way to the airport. As he boarded the plane at the back in Economy, he handed the oysters to a stewardess and asked her to put them in the plane's fridge so they would keep fresh.

She was horrified. Fortunately, a steward overheard the request and rushed over. "Oooh! Oysters, yummie!" he said. "I'll open them and serve them to you during the flight, if you like."

The steward couldn't have been more helpful, in contrast to the scowling stewardess. He invited Gus to sit in the lounge at the back of the plane—it must have been a DC6 or something ancient like that—while he served his oysters with a fine Chardonnay from First Class while the other Economy Class passengers had sandwiches.

One of the finest steaks Gus had ever eaten was in Economy Class served by a steward, not a female, on a flight from Las Palmas, Canary Islands, to San Juan, Puerto Rico. During the flight, he suddenly remembered he was carrying a cache of marijuana in the pocket of his jeans and realised he might be caught by customs. He wondered what to do, so he asked the young steward who rolled his eyes in exaggeration, put his finger to his lips and suggested he go the lavatory. "I'll come too," he said.

Together they shared the joint, and it made him feel he could have flown without the plane. That was probably what made the steak taste so good and the steward seem so obliging.

Now that he was old and semi-retired, Gus believed he deserved the perks of mature respectability. *Perhaps being old*, he thought as he looked out of the speeding plane's window, *is a bit like being drunk. You never quite know what you're doing even if you think you do.*

He was jerked from his reminiscing as the Boeing 777 lifted off the runway and headed east towards the Maldives. A flourish of flight announcements by the purser informed him of the languages spoken by the crew. He didn't care about that, but about the service. It was his experience with flying that when the purser heading the cabin crew was a woman, service would be poor. He reasoned it was because certain women, by their very nature, did not have the dedication to hospitality and enjoyment that men did. A man—whether steward or passenger—knows how to enjoy himself while flying; a woman, especially one who crosses herself during take-off, regards it as a chore, and a risky one at that.

As he feared, the champagne service was abominably slow and he wasn't offered more than one refill; the meal service abrupt—he had to request bread when the female flight attendant forgot to bring it—and somehow the all-female cabin crew conveyed the impression that whatever he asked for was an impertinence, even though he did get a large cognac just before landing. By then he was seething with exasperation, as well as being slightly tipsy.

He was first off the plane, holding up the other passengers as he took time to descend the staircase and hobbled across the tarmac to the arrivals hall. There were long queues at each of the immigration desks. Experience told him that whichever queue he joined would be the slowest moving one, and so it was. He was stuck behind a long line of pairs of backpack-hefting, poorly dressed couples in T-shirts and jeans, addressing each other in a guttural language he was glad he didn't understand.

He was upset at how ugly those people looked, in their

trusting twosomes of man and woman. What children would they breed when they themselves seemed so unloved and insecure? They clutched at each other, marched up to the Immigration desks together, and dutifully presented their passports in unison.

"You're here on business?" the immigration officer—a young lad with a beard and long eye lashes—asked Gus, because he had ticked that option on the 'Purpose for visit' section on the Immigration form. As well as Business, the choices were Holiday, Transit, Official, Employment and Other. While he would have liked some of the Other, he decided to be honest.

"Yes, just for three days."

The official raised his eyebrows. "Staying at Sunshine Island?"

"Yes, it's a new one."

The youth licked his lips under his scraggly beard and seemed to be in doubt. He looked up as a bulky woman stuffed into a uniform of khaki shirt and calf-length skirt, black socks and shoes, waddled up officiously. The youth said something to her and the woman, who reached up to Gus' chin in height, looked him up and down. He was wearing a neat safari suit made in Bangkok, of a weave of silk and linen. He looked rather smart, and hoped his appearance would convince the woman he was responsible enough to be allowed into the Maldives.

"On business? You need a visa in advance," she said with a haughty look of triumph.

"What? I've never had one before. Is this a new regulation?" Gus knew he had to bluff it out.

"He's been here before, many times," said the immigration chap in English, flicking through his passport.

"Of course I have," he said, forgetting the golden rule of never volunteering information to a uniformed official, since it would only lead to more questions. And more lies. "I live in Dubai, I come here often."

"On business?" The woman nodded her head ominously.

"Well," Gus said drawing back from the bottomless pit into which he suddenly realised he was about to step. "Not employment. I'm retired. I'm, er, on holiday, a short break. To see friends."

"Really?" The woman eyed him doubtfully.

"He says he's going to Sunshine," the immigration officer said, apparently trying to be helpful.

"It's a new resort, not properly open yet." Gus smiled wanly.

"You're going there on business?"

"No, not really." He guessed the woman was trying to set a trap. "I checked business on the form because I am only here for three days and the resort isn't properly open yet. It is a short holiday, actually. I'm not on business. My mistake. The owner's a friend." He was lying, he'd never met the owner, but hoped the bloody woman was convinced.

The woman said something in Dhivehi to the youth behind the counter and turned away to look for some other unfortunate tourist to harass.

"May I see your ticket?"

"Of course. It's only an email print out." Gus handed over the sheet of A4 paper he had himself printed up when he had made the flight booking via the Internet. "You see, I have a reservation to leave in three days."

"Yes." The young official's face was expressionless, and Gus wondered if that was because of the cameras on the pillars of the hall, or whether he really disliked him—or his job. He was relieved when he heard the reassuring thump of the rubber seal being stamped onto the last empty page of his passport.

"I'll have to get a new passport soon," he said to make conversation. "That's nearly full."

The youth said nothing and put the passport on the counter, his brows narrowing. "You must stay in our capital sometime," the youth suddenly said, as Gus reached for his passport. "That way you will learn about the real Maldives, our culture, our way of life. That's not possible in a resort."

Gus grabbed the passport, nodded his thanks and hurried across to the customs exit, where he put his overnight bag on the conveyor belt through the X-ray machine. He had no checked baggage since his visit was so short; and had not even bothered to bring his laptop. He retrieved the bag from the other side of the X-ray machine and began to walk towards the exit.

"Excuse me," said a girl no taller than a sack of rice. She wore a white tunic top over black trousers and her head was swaddled in white scarf fastened under her chin. "Is this all your luggage?"

"Yes," Gus said, trying desperately not to let his fury at being stopped and questioned again, by yet another officious female, give her satisfaction.

"Are you on business?"

He sighed with annoyance. "No, I'm just on a three-day visit. To stay with friends. At the new Sunshine resort." He remembered in time not to mention anything about being asked to design the resort's spa.

"Have you any books?"

"Only my sketch books."

"Sex books?" The girl looked startled.

"No," he said with an encouraging laugh so as not to cause her embarrassment. "*Sketch* books. I'm an artist."

Whether the girl believed him or not, she glanced behind

him, over his shoulder, where a male customs officer smiled at him as he turned and nodded his approval. The girl waved him on. "Welcome to Maldives," she said blankly. "Enjoy your holiday."

Gus made his way through the thicket of resort representatives brandishing boards with their resort or their guests' names on them, until he saw a lad holding a board with his name.

"That's me," he said with relief.

"Welcome to Maldives, Mr Augustus," said the Maldivian. "My name is Mohamed. I am your island host. You have no luggage?"

Gus waved his overnight bag and was surprised when the lad took it quickly from his hand.

"Please follow me," Mohamed said. "The launch is waiting."

On board the air-conditioned speed boat, with a cool, but soft, drink in his hand, served courteously by Mohamed, Gus began to relax. He knew he was often crotchety and biased, especially when women were involved as they always seemed to make things go wrong. He needed these few days in the resort to make him feel young and tolerant again.

He wondered why the owner had contacted him to design the resort's spa. He had designed other resorts in the islands but didn't fool himself into thinking it was because the owner liked his work. There was probably so little money left over after paying the outrageous fees of the resort's Californian architects, that Gus was all they could afford. He was cheap by their standards and happy to get away from his practice in Dubai to spend a couple of nights at the resort. The fact that it wasn't open appealed to him, since there would be no annoying female guests to put up with.

As Mohamed helped him from the launch onto the newly built arrivals jetty, a dazzling young blonde in a mini skirt, see-through blouse and apparently no bra, hugged him in welcome.

"I am Lizette," she said. "Mr Yevtushenko has instructed me to see you have everything you want during your stay at Sunshine."

Gus bristled with pleasure. As he looked around, another girl came forward with a chilled glass of champagne on a tray.

Gus accepted it eagerly, smiling at the girl. "Not Russian, I hope," he said, meaning it to be a joke.

"We are Russian," Lizette said. "The champagne is Krug."

"Yes, of course. Is Mr Yevtushenko here?"

"No. Unfortunately, he had to fly to Moscow. On business. You were already on your way, so we couldn't let you know. So he wants you to relax and enjoy Sunshine during your three days here. No business."

Gus's immediate reaction was one of extreme annoyance. He had flown at Yevtushenko's request (albeit at the Russian's expense) to discuss the spa he wanted designed, and the bugger wasn't there. On the other hand, as he followed Lizette along the sandy pathway, noticing the way her cute *derrière* in her tight mini-skirt sashayed from side to side, it might not be a waste of time…

As Lizette showed him the villas under construction, he barely took any notice as he was distracted by her deliberate flaunting of her provocative body.

There were only ten villas on the island and he observed that each one was extravagantly designed in a faux classical style with a parade of columns. As part of each lavish villa, there was a mosaic-lined swimming pool that looked like something from a 1950s Hollywood movie.

"This is your villa," Lizette said, when she opened the door in a wall and stood aside for him to enter. The first thing he saw was a swimming pool, under palm trees in the villa's garden.

"This pool is yours to enjoy," she said. "It is totally private. Would you like, how do you say, a dip?" Lizette tugged playfully at the top button of his safari shirt, deftly unfastening it.

Gus almost fainted. *It had been a long time.* "I have nothing to wear," he said, his voice suddenly husky.

"Then we bathe in the nudie!" Lizette suddenly stripped off her blouse, let her skirt fall to her feet and, with a laugh that was an invitation, jumped naked into the pool.

Gus, encouraged by the champagne, the sunshine, the intimate privacy of the villa and the sheer craziness of what was happening, unbuttoned his shirt, tore open his zippered fly, kicking off his trousers, underwear and shoes as though he were a randy teenager, and leapt into the pool to join her.

Later, lying naked in the sun with Lizette on a sunbed made for two, another glass of champagne in his hand, he no longer felt old. He vowed he would never let a woman, even a religious purser, an immigration official or a customs officer doing her job, upset him again. Women were wonderful.

With a smile, he recalled what he had thought on the plane: *Being old is a bit like being drunk. You never quite know what you're doing even if you think you do.*

"Life is fun," he announced to Lizette. "Just as it was when I was young." He held out his glass for Lizette to fill again. "I must make it my business never to forget that."

10. "See You Later, Alligator"

The driver manoeuvred the coach skilfully into the allotted space in the parking area. "Back here at four o'clock sharp," he shouted to his passengers, who were already pushing and shoving towards the exit.

"The coach park shuts at half-past four, so if you ain't here then, I go without you, right?"

But already the male employees from Better Rite Bathroom Ware, on their annual day-trip to the seaside, were leaping and whooping like school boys released from the classroom. Stan and Pete stood on the pavement, sniffing the air like dogs and, pulling their combs from the back pocket of their jeans, adjusted their quiffs and straightened their leather jackets. This action occurred every few minutes—it became a way of life, like breathing.

"What shall we do first?" asked Stan. "The beach?"

"Get some chips," replied Pete, "and then find the funfair."

"How much money have you got on you?" Stan enquired.

"Seven quid and a pocketful of change I nicked from my sister's money box," replied his mate. "What about you?"

"A tenner," boasted Stan. "My old man chucked me a couple of quid to buy him some whelks, and potted shrimps to take home for Ma."

"Cor," replied Pete, holding his nose, "you'll be stinking the coach out on the way home."

They laughed, combed their hair into place once more and,

like moths to a flame, made their way to the funfair.

The two teenage pals sauntered throughout the amusement park. Their new way of walking had been carefully copied from a recent film they had seen, where the 'baddie' had 'sauntered' his way through gangland before getting shot.

The cacophony of sounds from the whirling, twirling, dipping and diving rides excited them. It was as though every record on every jukebox was playing a different tune at the same time. They each purchased a cowboy hat, which they wore far back on their heads, ensuring their manicured quiffs stayed in place, but in danger of sliding off altogether due to an excess of Brylcream.

They called out, "Aye-aye" to the girls they passed, pretty girls in full dresses and a glimpse of petticoat at the hem. The girls would tip their chins into the air, shrug their shoulders at each other and roll their eyes, and walk past in so-called disgust. But they then turned, delighted and flattered, in giggling hope that the boys would follow them.

But Stan and Pete had more important things on their mind—finding girls could wait a while. The rides were calling them.

They went on the Waltzer and the Octopus. They rode the big dipper and the ghost train. They ogled, from the viewing gallery, the knickers and suspenders of the girls as they slid down the Stick Wall as the massive drum slowed. They went on the dodgems with Pete insisting on driving because he'd just got his motorbike licence. And that was where Stan saw her.

At first Stan thought she was a boy. She had short dark hair slicked back but no quiff. She was wearing a black jacket but her legs were concealed in the dodgem car in front of them, so he couldn't see if she was wearing jeans too, but it seemed likely.

"Hey, look at that," he said to Pete. "That a boy or girl?"

As if in answer, the dodgem car suddenly spun around and bashed their car full on. The driver shrieked with laughter as only a girl could, circled around their stalled car and gave the boys a cheeky wave before driving off.

"Stone me, it's a bint," said Stan. "Follow her, will you," he said, grabbing the steering wheel that Pete was clutching in surprise and spinning it around. "Step on it, you moron."

The car re-started in response to Pete's foot on the accelerator, and they began chasing the other car as the girl driving it waved mockingly at them. They almost caught up with her and were about to swipe her car on its side when the power stopped.

"Time up," bellowed a voice from the tannoy.

Stan watched to see if the girl was going to get out. "She's staying on!" he shouted to Pete. "Let's go for another round. I'll pay."

The power came on again and as they started up, a boy jumped on the back of their car and demanded payment. "Here y'are," said Stan. "I'll pay for the bloke, sorry bird, in that car too," he said.

Pete looked at his friend in disbelief. "Blimey, mate. Yer bleedin' mad."

"Just shut up and drive," said Stan. "That's crumpet, ain't it? And it bashed us. You know what that means?"

"No, what?" Pete was pressing his foot down to the floor trying to catch up with the girl's car.

"She's interested, mate, that's what. And she's by herself." He looked at Pete and winked. "Two's up?"

"Naah, ain't gonna happen."

To their astonishment, as they chased the car with the girl in it, she suddenly turned and headed straight for them again.

"She's playing chicken," said Stan. "Don't give way, Pete. Bash her." He grabbed the wheel to stop Pete steering out of the way of the on-coming car. The collision nearly threw both of them out of their seats.

"Suckers!" called the girl as she reversed and steered away from them.

"That's enough of that," said Stan. "She's bleedin' asking for it, mate. We've scored."

They cruised around the track but each time the girl in the car managed to steer out of their way. The power was switched off and the two of them got out of the car unsteadily. Stan looked around for the girl but the car she had been driving was empty.

"She can't have gone far," he said. "Come on, Pete. She's around here somewhere."

"You're not gonna chase after that, are you?" Pete said scornfully. "She's dressed like a boy!"

Stan took his comb out of his back pocket and carefully groomed his quiff back into shape. "But she ain't a boy, right?"

They trawled the fairground searching for her, Stan more enthusiastically than Pete.

"What you gonna do when you find her?" Pete grumbled.

"What do you think?" grinned his mate.

"Ere," said Pete, stopping in his tracks and lowering his voice. "Have you still got your—you know—" He glanced around to make sure nobody was listening, "—packet of three," he hissed.

"'Course I have," replied Stan. "Carry them with me all the time. Mind you," he continued, "it's a packet of two at the moment. I used one on that Beryl Baines in the factory bicycle shed during the Christmas social."

"Ah yes," mused Pete. "I've had her sister."

The boys were lying, of course. They had plucked up courage to each buy their first packet of Durex condoms two years previously, Stan being fortunate in being served by the male chemist, whilst Pete had the humiliation of bleating his order to the young female assistant. The two missing Johnnies had been experimented with, in the privacy of their bedrooms. Both boys were virgins.

A high-pitched laugh which they recognised came from the ride next to where they were standing.

"She's on the Waltzer," said Stan. As the tub in which she sat twisted and spun past them, the girl shouted, "See you later, alligator!"

They watched bemused, as her boyish, elfin face under that ridiculous hair cut zoomed past, ten, fifteen, twenty times. And then the ride slowed down and stopped, and the tub in which the girl had been sitting was empty.

"Gone again," sighed Pete. "Come on, mate, she's giving us the run-around."

"But I've got to find her," said Stan, in a panic.

"Why on earth?" asked his mate.

Stan, feeling embarrassed and totally bewildered pulled out his comb and put his quiff to rights. "I dunno, Pete," he replied. "I dunno why. But I've just *got* to."

They managed to sit behind her on the caterpillar ride. When the canopy came over, shielding all the riders from view of the spectators, Stan reached out and brushed his hand across the short sleek hair of the girl in the car in front of him. But when the canopy slowly rolled itself up and exposed the squealing, pretend-frightened passengers, she had gone again.

"I've had enough of this," moaned Pete. "Let's find

ourselves some decent crumpet. That is, if we can afford to treat them to a couple of rides and a bag of chips each. Blimey, Stan, we aren't 'arf getting through the dosh."

Stan grabbed his mate's arm and pointed. "Over there," he shouted. "By the rifle range. Look, she's waving to us."

"Yeah," replied Pete, "and by the time we get there she'll be gone again."

"Ssssh!" warned Stan. "She's coming over. Bloody hell, she's coming over!"

She stood before them, five foot nothing. Skinny. Hair like a boy. Dressed like a boy. Jeans, they noted, and an imitation leather jacket. But she had perfect white teeth and her nose wrinkled when she smiled. And she had freckles, like someone had flicked a paint-brush dipped in sepia at her. And her hair, once slicked back, had now fallen over her forehead in a wonderful quiff. Stan was smitten.

"What's your name?" he asked.

"Jacky," she replied, and he thought it was the best name in the world, even though it normally belonged to a boy.

"Will you try and win me a prize on this rifle range?" she asked. "Something for me to remember you by."

Stan, shouldering the pathetic gun, which surely had had its sights altered, aimed, fired and won. He chose a rather tacky little necklace. A thick chain from which dangled a tin alligator. He tied it around her neck, and she wrinkled her nose at him.

Suddenly Pete broke the spell by shouting, "Bleedin' hell! What's the time?"

Neither of the boys possessed a watch, but Jacky did. "It's twenty-five past six," she announced.

"We've missed the bloody coach," yelled Pete. "What the hell are we going to do?" He was silent for a moment. "I know,

110

I'll phone my old man to come and fetch us. But we'll have to wait till morning, he's on the night shift."

"Where the heck are we going to spend the night?" asked Stan, of no-one in particular. The three of them looked at each other.

"Tell you what," said Jacky, suddenly. "If you wait in the shelter at the far end of the esplanade, I'll pop back later with a couple of blankets and something to eat. Don't," she warned them, "stay in the fair ground. My Dad owns the place, and he has a security team out checking before they close down for the night. Just find that shelter by the beach and I'll be back, but it'll be late, after everyone's gone to bed."

She winked at Stan. "And I might as well bring a blanket for me, too."

She disappeared again while the boys thought about their situation. "My old man will go stark, raving mad," announced Pete, as they made themselves at home in the windowless and slightly smelly shelter Jacky had recommended, and sat on a bench.

"He'll be okay," replied Stan. "After all, he was young once," he said, quoting something he had once heard from an elder. But then he thought of something that made him sit up in horror. "Bloody hell, Pete," he shouted. "I forgot to get my old man his whelks and shrimps."

"We're in a right mess, we are," said Pete. "And all because of that bint."

"She's a bit of all right though, ain't she?" Stan said with a chuckle. "Makes me horny just thinking of her."

The two boys were silent as darkness crept over the esplanade. There was no light in the shelter and soon they couldn't see each other. Stan was grunting.

"What are you doing?" said Pete.

"I told you, I'm feeling horny. Give us a kiss!" Stan reached out and touched Pete's arm.

"What d'yer mean?" Pete was shocked.

"Just a joke, Pete. We'll have the real thing here soon."

"I don't know." Pete sounded worried. "There's something wrong."

"Don't worry," said Stan. "That Jackie's hot. She said she has to wait until people have gone to sleep. She's gonna bring food and blankets. You'll see."

Pete sucked on his lips with worry.

"Cor, are you blowing me a kiss, then?"

"Shut up," said Pete. "I tell you, I ain't happy. What the hell are we doing here, waiting for some bint to spend the night with us? Do you remember, she said her dad owns the fairground?"

"Yeah, I guess that's why she was having so many rides."

"But you paid for one, didn't you? And you paid at the rifle range."

"Why not?"

"You see where it's got us. We missed the coach and we're stuck here. She ain't gonna come, you know."

"Oh Pete, don't worry. We're gonna have a great time, even if my dad's gonna go crazy. No bloody whelks."

In spite of their bravado, the two boys were beginning to feel foolish. Gradually they both fell silent as they stretched out on the benches and tried to sleep. Pete was trying to puzzle out why he had let his mate talk him into this situation. *If Stan hadn't followed that bird,"* he thought, *we would have watched the time and caught the coach home.*

Pete suddenly sat up. "Something's wrong," he said aloud.

"What's that? Cor, I must have dozed off," said Stan.

"Stop pulling yer puddin', Stan, and think. This ain't kosher. We ought to get out of here."

"Get out? Not bloody likely," said Stan. "I've spent all the dough anyway."

"On that bint."

"Yeah," said Stan. Perhaps she'll lend us some?" He chuckled. "I'll ask her when she comes." He looked in Pete's direction as a flashlight lit up the shelter.

"Hey up, mate," he said happily. "Here she comes." He pulled his comb from his pocket and slowly combed his quiff into place.

#

The car park hasn't changed at all, thought Stan as the driver opened the doors of the coach and released his cargo of excited men onto the tarmac. They leapt and whooped and playfully wrestled each other, before dispersing in groups of two, three or more, to discover the attractions and temptations of the seaside town.

Stan was the last to leave the coach. He didn't leap or shout. As he was now the Manager of the Despatch Department at Better Rite Bathroom Ware, he didn't feel it would be suitable for him to draw attention to himself. Anyway, he didn't feel much excitement.

Eighteen years, he thought to himself in amazement. *Eighteen bleedin' years ago I was here with Pete.*

"Coming to the pub, Stan?" yelled one of a quartet of men, dressed unbecomingly for their age in jeans and T shirts with tacky slogans.

"Naah," replied Stan. "I'll catch you later. Got to pace

meself," he said to put them off. He wondered why the hell his firm had chosen the resort for this year's annual 'Merry Men's Day Trip to the Sea'. Even the title 'Merry Men' filled him with disgust; it made them sound like a group of Morris Dancers, or homos.

Stan made his way to the funfair. The tinny music had changed its tune. As he passed by each ride, he found it difficult to decipher each blast of sound. He stood and gazed around.

The massive drum of the Stick Wall had gone, and in its place was a terrifying ride which lifted its line of strapped-in passengers higher than high, and then seemingly dropped them, screaming and retching, to the ground. The Waltzer was still there. And the Octopus. But the Ghost Train was now the House of Fun. And the dodgems were still there. Stan stood and watched the cars as they bumped and jostled each other, and the boys, showing off, drove with one hand whilst the girls beside them feigned terror.

This was the last ride I went on with Pete, he mused. *This is where I met that girl with the daft hairdo.*

He had stopped thinking about her many years ago, but now he wondered where she was, what she was doing. No good wondering about Pete, though. Pete had ceased to be. He had bought himself a knackered old motor bike soon after he got his driving licence. On his first drive out, he didn't return to the café where Stan and his mates were waiting. The police came instead to break the news that there had been an accident on the motorway and Pete had been killed.

I need a beer, thought Stan. *Got to get away from this bleedin' fun fair.*

He turned his back on the noise and crowds and donut smells and headed to the esplanade, where there were a few little shops selling trinkets and mementos, and the odd chippy and a café. He hoped to find a bar. Stopping in front of a seedy, urine-smelling shelter, he realised that this was the place where he and Pete had spent the night eighteen years before.

He remembered how, wrapped in thin blankets and eating the sad sandwiches that the girl had brought them, he couldn't believe his luck. Soon after she arrived, he had told poor Pete to 'take a walk'. This was the shelter where he had lost his virginity.

"I need a beer," he thought, again.

The line of small shops and kiosks came to an end. No pub. But the last building was a bright looking café with tables placed outside and a good menu chalked on a board. He decided to get pissed later on, as he realised, he was very hungry. Trying to memorise the awkward order that he'd decided upon, Stan, at the front of the queue at last, found himself staring into the face of the girl behind the counter.

A face with freckles and a nose that wrinkled when she smiled at him, and spiky hair, dyed orange. His mind went blank and he found himself saying, "Jacky?"

The girl laughed. "I'm not Jacky. It's my Mum you want." She called out, "Mum, there's a man here wants you," and leaving Stan to stand to one side, she moved on to serve another customer.

Jacky and Stan stared at each other. At first, she didn't recognise him, but slowly her puzzled frown went, and she said, "Christ almighty!"

She lifted a flap in the counter and beckoned him to come through. He followed her into a small stock room. Sitting on boxes of baked beans and paper towels they took stock of each other.

She hasn't changed so very much, thought Stan. Her hair was different, longer and with a fringe. She had put on weight. She wore a blue overall, but he noticed, around her neck, a thin pretend silver chain from which dangled a tin alligator.

"How's life treating you?" he asked, sounding pathetic.

"Oh, mustn't grumble," she replied. "Dad retires this year and he's giving over the ownership of the funfair to me and my husband."

"Husband?" he said, not knowing what else to say.

"Oh yes. I married one in a million." She smiled. "It's not everyone who would take on a girl with a baby."

"Baby?" he asked, and realised he was sounding like a parrot.

"Yes, Stan. I had a baby. And before you ask, no, it's not yours. You used a condom, remember? What a fuss you made putting it on. It's Pete's. When you'd finished and fell asleep, Pete came back and had a go. He didn't bother with a condom. I called her Petra, after him. Is he okay?"

Stan put his head in his hands. "He died soon after we came here. Motorbike accident."

Jacky stirred herself and, standing up, said, "Well, take care of yourself, Stan." Leaving him to collect his thoughts she disappeared through the door towards the customers awaiting their orders.

He sat for a few minutes, pulled himself together then left the store room.

"Aren't you going to order?" asked the spiky haired girl, who was Petra.

"No, love," he said. "Another time perhaps."

"Okey-dokey," she replied. "See you later... alligator."

He turned, smiled at Pete's daughter... and went to find a pub.

11. Gideon

The sounds from the camper van, parked in a clearing just off-road and beneath a small Welsh mountain, were horrific. Thumps, bumps, clumps. The van rocked alarmingly as something heavy made contact with the side door. A frying pan sailed from the open window on the passenger side and landed in a thorn bush. The language coming from within the vehicle was modern-day Anglo Saxon. Polly and Martin were having a row.

The entire journey from Essex to Snowdonia had been fraught with tension. The satnav undoubtedly had been lying and Polly obviously had been reading the map upside-down. The pre-booked holiday park was nowhere to be found, and now it had started to rain, daylight was fading, and it seemed they would have to spend the night beside the road at the back of beyond.

Polly screamed, "I'm leaving you now!" opened the door and stepped from the hired camper van with as much dignity as she could muster.

"Good riddance!" yelled Martin, throwing her backpack through the door for her to pick up. He started the engine and, without giving her a chance to get back in, leaned over, pulled the door closed and drove back onto the road.

#

The rain had become a deluge. Polly found that her anger was rapidly evaporating, and she was becoming rather frightened and sorry for herself. Her hair hung in rat tails and dripped down the back of her jersey. Her feet, in her inadequate sandals, were squelching in the puddles, and her legs were cold and saturated. Her backpack hung on her shoulders, getting heavier at each step.

She had no torch and the new moon, like a pale lemon fingernail, gave no illumination whatsoever. Polly trudged along the road keeping to the grass verge to guide her. *Surely*, she thought, *Martin would have turned round by now, and driven back to find me?*

But no, she had been abandoned on an unknown road in an unknown wilderness, and she was soaking wet and frightened and now she was crying.

As she screwed up her eyes against the deluge of rain, Polly saw a distant light. She stumbled along for what seemed an eternity, until she reached the building, the only one she could see beside the road. A refuge. And she could hear laughter coming from within.

The customers of the 'Three-Legged Goat' had reluctantly relinquished their coveted Dart Player of the Year cup to the 'Frog in Rapture' pub in the neighbouring village.

The Goats were now consoling themselves for their defeat in a free round of drinks from the pub's landlord. Conversation was muted, and rather nasty, and muttered from corners of mouths. The term 'jammy bastards' was used often.

Suddenly the pub door swung open and a dripping apparition staggered into the public bar. "Please, can you help me?" whispered Polly, as she fainted onto the beer-stained carpet.

Polly became gradually aware of hushed voices. She opened her eyes and found she was gazing up at a circle of worried and bemused, whiskered faces. She discovered that she had been placed on a low velveteen covered chair, with her legs and feet stretched out on a matching seat. She was enveloped in a rather smelly and hairy blanket. Struggling to get up, Polly found that not one ounce of energy remained in her body.

"Now, now my lovely," said a soothing sing-song voice. "It seems we've got ourselves a wee bit lost, haven't we?" A large and smiling woman, wearing a flowered apron and her hair in a bun, gently eased Polly to her feet.

"We'll run you a hot bath, my lovely," she said, "and get you out of those wet clothes and into one of my spare nighties, and we'll get you all tucked up in bed."

Polly was too tired to wonder who the 'we' could be.

"I'm Bronwen Evans," explained the motherly woman. "Landlady of this pub."

"But…" began Polly.

"You tell Bronwen all about it in the morning," she said, urging Polly to be quiet. "Lucky I am, that the guest room is already made up. Now," she ordered, "bath, bed, and I'll bring you up a nice bowl of soup." Putting her arm around Polly's shoulders she helped her through the bar and up the narrow stairs.

#

Polly woke with a start. She opened her eyes and stared at the ceiling, in the grey light of morning that filtered through a gap in the curtains. For a moment she was puzzled, wondering about the strangeness of her surroundings. She wasn't in the flimsy bed of the camper van, and she seemed to be alone. As the memory of what had happened the night before gradually penetrated her befuddled brain, she sat up in alarm. "Oh dear," she said to herself. "What have I done?"

As if in answer, the was a knock on the door which opened quickly. A hand switched the light on and Polly found herself gazing up at the friendly face of a middle-aged woman, wearing a red cardigan and a bonnet secured under her chin with a bow. She carried a tray on which was a steaming mug of tea.

"Are you all right, my lovely?" the woman asked. "I'm Bronwen, you remember."

"Yes," Polly whispered, feeling thoroughly ashamed at the situation she had got into. "I'm sorry about last night. I didn't mean to cause any trouble."

"You didn't, my lovely. I'm glad you found us. There's a lot of bad people out there. This is our guest room. I've dried your clothes, they're in the bathroom, so you can get up, have a wash and you'll feel as right as rain."

"Rain?" Polly giggled. "It was the rain that caused it," she said. "We were lost. Had a row. I ran away. In the rain. How stupid of me."

"It was a bit, but I suppose you had a reason." Bronwen sounded sympathetic. "You weren't being chased, were you? Did someone try to harm you?"

"Oh no. Just my boyfriend being awkward so I left him. But he was in the camper van, and I was in the rain and had no idea where I was. I thought he'd come after me and beg me to get back in the van. We were supposed to be going on holiday. To a campsite by the beach."

"Men!" said Bronwen. "You're lucky to be rid of him."

"Really?" Polly didn't like that idea. "How will he get on without me?"

"The same way he did before he met you."

"But we've been living together for a year."

"Probably a year of your life wasted."

"I must phone him." She reached for her backpack which was on the floor beside the bed, pulled out her smart phone and pressed the button for his number. She waited a minute, while Bronwen shook her head in disapproval.

"There's no reply," Polly said. "His battery must be flat."

"Yes," said Bronwen. "unless he doesn't want to answer you. Now drink your tea. I have to go the market. The bathroom's at the end of the hall. The kitchen's downstairs. You'll find my husband there. You can help him do the dishes."

"Oh yes, of course. You are so kind. I don't know how to repay you."

"Twenty pounds will do. It's usually twenty-five pounds for bed and breakfast for this room but that's for a couple, which you're not. I won't charge you for last night's soup, my lovely."

Polly was speechless. She hadn't expected a bill.

After finding her clothes and getting dressed, Polly made her way down the stairs to the kitchen behind the bar, following the sound of pots and crockery rattling. *Thank goodness*, she thought with relief, *the three most essential possessions—the three Ms: money, mobile and make-up—I need for this predicament are safely stowed in my backpack.*

She hoped there would be a bank or post office in the village, although (scary thought), perhaps the Three-Legged Goat was the only building for miles around as she hadn't seen any lights from houses the night before. Entering the kitchen, she was greeted by a massive, smiling man who stood at the sink, looking ridiculous in a 1940s style pinny which strained against his enormous belly.

"Hello, bach," he grinned. "I'm the landlord, husband of Bronwen. I'm Evan Evans."

Polly stopped herself in time from remarking "Good

'eavens."

He threw a tea towel at her and said, "I'll wash, you wipe."

In just a few minutes Evans had elicited almost the entire history of Polly's life. She was twenty-two, she lived in Chelmsford, Essex. She had an older sister. She worked as a medical secretary at a teaching hospital. She had just dumped her boyfriend. She would never trust any man again, not ever.

The information Polly gleaned from Evan was that the nearest village with a post office was a four mile walk away, and that there were no buses that passed by the Goat pub. With the washing up completed and the kitchen tidied, Polly resolved to take things easy, think things over and see what she should do next. She decided to go for a walk.

Polly had never before seen such a beautiful, idyllic place. She was delighted by the traditional appearance of the pub, constructed of red brick with a thatched roof. The sign of the three-legged goat made her laugh. There was a duck pond with an overhanging willow and a field with cows and, astonishingly, a goat!

The road was a narrow, sandy track. Wild flowers grew amongst the hedgerows. And there was a church. In fact, as Polly quickly realised, the hamlet boasted just the two buildings, pub and church. No cottages. The pub's customers obviously lived in nearby farms and drove to and from the pub and church.

The last time Polly had been inside a church was four years previously, when she had been chief bridesmaid at her sister's wedding. For now, having just a peep inside this tiny, flint-stoned building with its minute tower, seemed the most important thing in the world. She opened the lynchgate, and began to walk towards the church's ancient wooden door. Abruptly, she stopped, her heart thumping against her chest.

Sitting on top of a grave, staring at her with a look she couldn't decipher, was a man. He was, she immediately decided, beautiful. He was dressed rather oddly, in tight trousers tied below the knees with string, a strange dark blue shirt, a red neckerchief, and a weird straw hat.

"Oh," stammered Polly, "I'm most dreadfully sorry, am I trespassing? You see, I only arrived last night and…"

The man stood up, stared at her, and walked away, around the side of the church and out of sight.

Oh, thought Polly, *how bloody rude!* She made her way back to the pub, to find the place was in chaos.

Evan Evans was running around the bar like a headless chicken. Another man, younger and equally distraught was yelling, "Ma, Ma, are you all right Ma?"

Bronwen Evans was stretched out upon two pub tables, showing her knickers to the world and groaning in pain. Her right leg was in a rather strange position.

Polly quickly took stock of the situation. "She's broken her leg," she diagnosed. "I'm a medical secretary, and I know about these things. Evan," she said, "phone for an ambulance, and you," she pointed to the young man, who was obviously the son, "stop flapping and get a blanket and cushion for her." They jumped to her command.

Later, when Bronwen had been dispatched to the local cottage hospital, ("I always told her not to stand on that ladder to get to the crisps," had said Evan) Polly found she had a job. One of the credentials she had confessed to the landlord during the washing up period at The Goat was that her parents ran a pub in Essex. Also, that she was a dab hand behind the bar during her time off work. Evan was flabbergasted when she offered to help and accepted immediately.

Her first night behind the bar at the 'Goat' was a huge success. The customers loved her strange accent and her flirty chat. They admired the stern frown she gave them when they tried to trick her by offering the incorrect amount for their drinks. They ogled her tight T-shirt. And they went home immediately when she called, "Last orders!"

Later, as she and Davey (oh, she discovered, the son was named Davey, and he had the bluest eyes ever) shared a well-deserved after-hours beer, she decided that she would stay on at the 'Three-Legged Goat' until Bronwen returned. Looking at Davey, she mused that she could, perhaps, return home and give a week's notice to quit her job at the hospital in Essex.

As though reading her thoughts, Davey asked, "How do you like it around here?"

"It's lovely," she replied. "But I met a very rude man in the church graveyard. He turned his back on me and walked away."

Davey went silent, took her empty glass from her hand and replaced it on the bar. Kissing her cheek like an older brother would, he quietly said, "Oh, you must have met Gideon—or rather *he* must have met *you.*"

Whatever did he mean by that? she asked herself when, tired after the events of the day, she lay in her small bed trying to sleep. She had been assigned a staff bedroom by Evans, who told her the guest room she had slept in the night before, had to be available for paying guests or customers who were too drunk to drive home.

She was intrigued by the mysterious Gideon and assumed he was the church caretaker. *Perhaps he is shy*, she thought, forgiving him his apparent rudeness. *He must have been scared out of his wits to see a total stranger in his church yard.* She wondered what Martin would say.

Martin. She hadn't thought of him all day. He hadn't even tried to phone her. *Wasn't he worried about her? Apparently not.*

As she drifted off to sleep, she found she was thinking of Davey and the comforting kiss he had given her in the bar. He seemed a sweet lad. She would enjoy working in the pub with him.

Early the next morning, she was woken by a rapid tap on her door. "I'm going to the hospital to see Bronwen," Evan Evans shouted from the hall. "Can you help Davey in the bar this morning? There won't be much business. Sometimes it's only old Dai Jones come for his daily couple of pints."

"Happy to do so, Evans," she called out, scrambling to get out of bed. She checked her mobile, but there was no message from Martin. She didn't worry about calling her parents as they didn't expect her back for a week as she was on holiday. She would tell them later what had happened, if she really decided to become a permanent member of the Three-Legged Goat pub staff.

Davey instructed her on the routine of getting the public and saloon bars ready for the day's customers. He showed her where spare glasses for spirits and beers were kept, and pointed out the shelf with the pint mugs reserved for regulars. He explained how the barrels for draught beer were stored in the cellar and either he or his dad would change them when necessary.

"Ma usually does sandwiches, you know, cheese and ham and pickled onions for lunch. I don't know what we'll do now."

His blue eyes, as he looked at her, made her heart skip a beat.

"Don't worry, Davey," she said, touching his arm. "I'm happy to help out. I just need a few days to understand where things are and who the customers are."

"You really mean you'll stay? It's so lonely here, we find it difficult to get help."

"I'd love to." She busied herself drying a glass.

"Depends on Ma," he said.

"Well, she won't be able to work for a few weeks with her leg in plaster, will she?"

Customers began to troop in. "It's busier than usual at lunch time," Davey said, as he pulled a beer and Polly poured a measure of whisky from the optics. "That's because you're here. They all want to see who the new barmaid is."

Polly was rushed off her feet, making sandwiches in the kitchen, collecting dirty glasses, doing the cash, but she soon fell into a rhythm with Davey and the two of them worked well together. It was almost closing time, when she got a chance to chat with a customer who had been in the bar since opening time.

"I'm Dai Jones," he had told her as he explained which beer mug was his. "I'm the oldest person who comes here," he said, when she walked over to him as they prepared to close. "And you must be the youngest barmaid I've ever met. Prettiest too."

"Cheeky!" she said, wiping the counter in front of him. "You must know everybody in the village," she added as a way of making conversation.

"Aye, I do that."

"So tell me, Dai. Who's Gideon?"

Suddenly, the chatter in the pub ceased. Polly felt all eyes were on her.

Polly stared, aghast, as the punters slowly turned their backs on her and sipped the remaining dregs of their pints. Even Dai Jones drained his glass, giving Polly a look of reproach. Muttering to each other in Welsh, they left the pub in a group, the last man closing the door firmly behind them. The silence was heavy, and Polly felt tears running down her cheeks.

"Oh Davey," she sobbed, "what on earth have I done? What have I said? Oh dear, they hate me."

Davey took her in his arms, and smoothed her hair and wiped her eyes. "They don't hate you, my lovely girl. It's just that you... er... well, you've sort of... er..."

Polly pulled herself out of his arms and snapped, "It's obvious that I have upset all your regulars. I shall go home tomorrow!"

Davey moved away from her and went behind the bar, where he started wiping glasses. "Please don't go, Polly," he said quietly. "We need you to help behind the bar while Ma is laid up, and, well, we just *need* you..."

"Oh," she retorted angrily, "You want me to stay until Bronwen is on her feet again, do you?"

He came to her side, took her hands in his and whispered, "Polly, bach, *I* need you!"

As she gazed into those blue, blue eyes, she thought she would drown in them.

Davey tore his gaze away and said "Go and sit down, lovely. I'll get us both a glass of brandy. We could do with it and no mistake."

They sat opposite each other on a wooden settle, neither speaking. They sipped their drinks, making them last, willing time to stand still.

"It's Gideon, isn't it?" she asked.

Davey sighed. "Yes, Polly. It's Gideon."

She reached across the table for his hand. "Tell me, Davey," she begged. "Who is Gideon?"

But he stood up, collected their glasses, and said, "Dad will be back soon so it'll be less work for us here tonight. Go'n have a rest. I'll tell you about Gideon when we have free time in the morning, my lovely girl." He kissed her on the cheek, propelled her to the door leading to the stairs and her room, and treated her to a wonderful smile that she couldn't decipher.

#

The next morning, as Evan Evans and his son prepared the bar for the lunchtime invasion of dedicated drinkers, Polly, in the kitchen, made piles of cheese and pickle sandwiches, and hard-boiled some eggs which she halved and placed prettily on a platter surrounded by lettuce and snipped chives.

Rummaging in the cupboards and larder (obviously the pride of Bronwen), she found flour and lard and made some pastry, which she then cut into little rounds and topped with cheese and tomato and baked as minute pizzas. These she displayed on another large dish. Oh, she didn't attend cookery classes for nothing!

As she placed her offerings on the bar, the eyes of Evan and Davey lit up. "Oh, bach," said Evans in amazement. "You can teach my wife a thing or two." Polly thought that was *not* a good idea but kept quiet.

Davey, who had been noticeably silent during the evening shift the day before, suddenly said, "We've got a good hour before we open, lovely. Shall we go for a walk?"

Polly mouthed the question "Gideon?" and Davey nodded.

They tramped, the pair of them, away from the pub and beyond the duck pond, skirted the cow field, (threw an old cabbage to the goat) and came to a stop at the church. The entire walk had been in silence, but they had held hands. They now sat on a large but comfortable gravestone, which stated in crumbling lettering that the remaining relics of the Smitherson family would be 'Looking forward to meeting up in glory'.

Polly, gazing at Davey, said, "Gideon. Tell me about that rude young man in the strange clothes. Who on earth is he, and why do the locals fear him?"

Davey, not looking at her, began slowly. "Gideon," he said, "is one hundred and forty years old. His family owned the Three-Legged Goat. He was in love with a local lass, Mairwen Morgan, but she was married to Alwyn Griffith, a brute of a man. Mairwen got pregnant by Gideon, but Alwyn found out about the affair and arranged to meet Gideon to 'fight to the death' in the woods behind the Church.

"Mairwen, poor girlie, begged her husband and her lover not to fight over her. It was to be fisticuffs. The men got stripped to their waists, and the fight began. But two pistol shots rang out, and two people lay dead."

Polly snuggled closer to Davey and quietly said, "So, Gideon shot Mairwen and Alwyn?"

"No," replied Davey, sadly and with head bowed. "Alwyn shot his wife and then Gideon."

Polly shivered slightly as Davey stood up and said, "I think we'd better be getting back to the pub. Pa will be all on his own."

But Polly pulled him down again. "So…" she said slowly, "the young man I saw was a ghost?"

"Yes," admitted Davey, quietly. "Every time a new, pretty woman arrives in the village, then our Gideon will appear to take a look at her to see if she is Mairwen. He soon goes away again."

Davey took her to see a grave; the headstone, surrounded in ivy and weed. The epitaph was almost indecipherable. But she read 'GIDEON OWEN LLEWELLYN, BAR-MAN. BORN 1860. DIED 1884. BELOVED SON.' And beside the grave was another, just a hump of earth, no stone, no words. "We like to think this could be Mairwen," said Davey.

They walked solemnly back to the pub. "Will I ever be accepted here?" she asked Davey.

"When they see that array of food you left on the bar, you'll soon be one of us," he laughed. "Don't worry, we're a funny old lot around here and, in your favour, Gideon only shows himself to the pretty women."

As they approached the pub, a man suddenly stepped out of the doorway with a scowl on his face.

"Martin!" Polly stared at him in surprise. He looked rather silly as he faced them, legs astride, arms akimbo. She wondered in an instant what she had ever seen in him.

"Oh," he remarked with sneer, observing Polly's hand entwined with Davey's. "Didn't take you long to find another man, did it? I didn't go far, I waited to see what you'd do. It was easy to trace you here, everyone around here is talking about the new bar maid at The Goat."

"I tried to phone you…"

"Oh, shut up! I'm finished with you." He pushed past them and made his way to the car park where Polly saw he had parked the camper van.

"*Hwyl fawr*… goodbye," said Davey with a chuckle.

"*Dim gwerth rhech dafad,*" Polly said slowly.

Davey, astonished by her comment, turned to Polly as Martin drove away. "Do you know what you've just said in Welsh? You just told your boyfriend he's 'not worth a sheep's fart'."

"Oh yes," smiled Polly. "I've been practising." She waved her smart phone at him. "Google told me what to say. And he's my ex-boyfriend now."

They laughed, because they both suddenly realised, they were in love.

12. The Devil's Gigolo

It was not Raju's career decision to become a gigolo.

Like everything else that happened to Raju, it just happened. That was his philosophy about life, if he thought about it, which he didn't. "I just go with the flow," he would say, if any of his friends asked him. He was content that way, he always had been.

From a young age, when strangers patted his head (which he hated), and said what a beautiful little boy he was, he knew he was special.

Nobody could see through him and yet everyone tried to. He kept his real self well hidden, having learned that the comment on his beauty brought benefits if he said nothing. His smile was enough; his perfect white teeth framed by his dark, voluptuous lips, enchanted people. He didn't know why; he didn't understand what it was that inspired people to trust him, help him, desire him. It happened.

It was as he progressed through childhood that he became aware of what he perceived as his special difference from other children. He was darker in complexion than any of them. While the fair ones, instructed by their mothers, sought to keep out of the sun, sitting in the shadow of trees on the river bank, he didn't care. He loved the river and swam in it all day whenever he could, delighting in the feel of the sun caressing his body. *I'm darker than anyone,* he would think to himself. *That's why I'm special.*

His parents—his father earned his living by climbing palm

trees to pluck coconuts; his mother did laundry at the river for other people—never worried about him. It was as though they too knew he was special, and that he would come to no harm whatever happened.

He had the usual adventures and misadventures of a young boy, learning by trial and error the code of god-fearing adults. He soon understood what belonged to others could not be his unless given to him.

He had no idea where his irresistible charm came from, but it worked like magic. Whatever he wanted he seemed to get: food from neighbours when he was hungry, sweets from other children when he turned his eyes wide on them, victory at sports. He found parrot-learning easy, passed school exams effortlessly. He won his teachers' praise, and the admiration of fishermen when he brought up a haul of crayfish from diving in the river.

His neighbours in the huts by the river bank regarded him as a lucky child and he liked that. As he grew older, he helped them in their chores, happy to be thanked, whether it was for steering buffaloes to plough the water-logged paddy fields to plant rice seedlings, or helping the baker to knead dough to make bread. Whatever he did for people was a success; the rice grew well; the bread baked perfectly and sold quickly.

At sixteen, he was a sturdy young chap with long, dark hair falling to his shoulders; his body taut and lean, his muscles honed by hard work in the paddy fields, hauling in fishing nets and climbing palm trees like his father, to pluck nuts for people who paid him. He gradually became aware that his body, beauty and charm were assets that brought rewards, especially when he gave in to the demands of village girls who inveigled him into their huts when their parents were out working. He learned quickly what they wanted and was happy to oblige. *What happens,*

happens.

So Raju was not surprised when a woman on holiday from Germany, beckoned him into her rented cabana in a coconut grove by the river and asked him to give her a massage. He accepted the twenty dollars she gave him as a reward with a broad grin that had the woman squealing and begging him to come again the next day. His career had begun.

#

Over the months, the people in the riverine village where Raju lived became accustomed to the sight of the occasional female tourist walking nonchalantly along the river bank, shielding her eyes as she studied the distant mountains, but surreptitiously glancing towards the cluster of huts. When the villagers saw the woman pause where Raju was draped invitingly on the trunk of a fallen palm tree, they smiled, nodded knowingly, proud of their star inhabitant, their Raju.

Raju's mother and father were at first troubled by the amount of hero-worship their only son was attracting from strangers. While his visits to the huts of the local girls ceased, something else was happening. Foreign women of all ages seemed to be seeking out Raju. His mother ignored the gossip as she did the laundry in the river, and his father greeted the knowing chuckles of the fishermen with a louder laugh. Gradually his parents became proud that Raju's good nature and eagerness to make people happy was winning him foreign women friends and bringing in dollars.

#

Raju hung his brightly-patterned beach shorts and T-shirt on a bush and jumped into the river, well away from his mother slapping clothes on stones to beat the dirt from them. He was naked, as usual when he bathed, and was enjoying being alone. The previous evening had been more demanding than he expected, as the woman who had invited at him to dinner had asked him so many questions about himself. He found it a strain, not only having to make conversation but also having to be careful to follow correct etiquette when dining in the hotel. But he managed and the woman seemed delighted, slipping a hundred-dollar bill into his hand as he left her room.

"Oh, those women!" he smiled to himself, as he floated in the river. "They are so kind and generous, and so eternally grateful."

As he lay on his back, keeping himself afloat with the minimum of movement, letting the water ride over his body, soothing his aching limbs, he became aware of someone shouting his name. Surprised at being disturbed in the morning, he glanced at the river bank and saw a man in a dark suit, and somewhat red in the face, waving at him.

"You are Raju?" the man bellowed.

He flipped over and struck out strongly for the shore. He scrambled up the river bank and stood naked and unfazed in front of the man.

"I am Raju, sir," he said.

The man looked confused. "Don't you have a towel or something?"

"Sure." Raju reached behind the man to where his shorts were hanging. "Shall I get dressed?"

"Please do." The man turned his back politely.

"What do you want?" Raju pulled on the shorts and flung his

T-shirt around his shoulders. He had never seen a man in a suit by the river before. He guessed he had come from the city and parked his vehicle on the main road, walking through the palm trees to the river. "How can I help?"

The man coughed as though about to say something with which he did not personally approve or agree. "I have been commissioned by a lady who is mightily interested in you." He paused and looked at Raju, who showed no surprise whatsoever.

"She has assigned me to find you and ask if you would like to be employed by her."

"*Employed?*" Raju was intrigued. He had never been employed before and was not sure if he would like it.

"She asks what your, er, charges are?"

Raju was perplexed. "Charges? I don't charge, I like to help people... the fishermen, the farmers, the village baker..."

The man sighed. "Don't try to be clever with me, young man. Women pay you money, don't they, for certain services?"

"Do you mean those gifts foreign women give me? How do you know about that?"

"You had dinner with a lady last night. She would like you to join her staff on a contract basis. She is prepared to offer you a thousand dollars a week."

"To do what?"

The man shrugged his shoulders. "Only you know. Just be yourself, I guess. You must travel with her tonight. Don't bother to pack anything, she will buy all you need. You must make your mind up now. Do you play, or do you stay?"

"Play?" Raju stared at the man, his brain racing. He was shocked. Was it a game when he helped people, did what they asked? He looked beyond the man through the trees and saw what must be his limousine parked on the road. Another man, the driver perhaps, was leaning against the car's bonnet, staring at them. He looked impatient.

For the first time in his life, instead of letting what happens happen, Raju made a decision. "I don't play," he said, challenging the man with hardened eyes. "I'll stay."

"What?" The man seemed astonished.

"Yeah, why not? I belong here. I do as I please, when I want. I help people, that's my life. It's not a game."

"Is it the money? She might pay double."

Raju turned away from the man, brushing his hand aside as he tried to stop him. "Go back to the city in your posh limousine," he said. "My life is my life."

He tossed his head, sending his wet hair fluttering and his T-shirt falling to the ground. He walked angrily back to the river. He paused for a moment as the man shouted, then plunged into the water, deliberately creating enough spray to splash the man. He swam to the middle of the river, turned on his back and waved.

Somehow, he knew he was doing more than waving goodbye to the man and, thus, to the woman who had sent him in a chauffeur-driven limousine. He was waving farewell to his youth, to his innocence, to his carefree life of freedom. He realised as he waved that he was taking control of his life.

He swam slowly with the river's flow, to where his mother and other village women were washing clothes. He emerged from the water beside his mother, his shorts dripping wet, and picked up her heavy basket of washed sheets and pillow cases, lifted it to his shoulders and, without a word, set off in the direction of home. His mother smiled her thanks, while the other women nodded happily at what a good boy Raju was.

His father was at home when he arrived, sitting on his

haunches in front of the hut, sharpening a hunting knife. He looked up anxiously. "There was a man asking for you," he said. "From the city."

Raju nodded. "He offered me *employment*."

"That's good."

"I told him I didn't want it."

His father sighed. "You can't live like this for ever, Raju. Just, well, drifting."

"I can climb trees to pluck coconuts as you get too old. I can help the fishermen, I can drive bullocks to plough the paddy fields."

"That's not what I mean. Those foreign women…"

Raju shook his head firmly, showing he had made a decision. "They can go to hell!"

#

The villagers soon noticed that something had changed in Raju. Word had spread among them about the man in the dark suit who had come in a limousine and spoken to him. Since then, Raju no longer hung about on the river bank but always seemed to be busy at something, whether setting traps for wild boar with his father, running errands for his mother, or diving in the river to spear crayfish. He seemed as cheerful as usual, always ready to help when needed, but there was something different. He was avoiding the women on vacation who came looking for him.

Even Old Nico, the feared food and beverage manager of the five-star hotel near the village, noticed the change in Raju.

On a visit to the river bank to purchase fresh crayfish for the hotel, he saw Raju sitting on his favourite tree trunk, relaxing after diving. He sat down uninvited beside him, taking out a packet of cigarettes and offering him one.

Raju was intrigued about why the man that the hotel staff and villagers were scared of because he was so mean, was trying to be friendly. "No thanks," he said with a modest smile of apology, "I don't smoke."

"You don't mind if I do?" Nico asked. "I don't get much chance at work."

"Of course not."

Nico lit the cigarette, puffed on it and then said casually, "We don't see you at the hotel any more. The guests miss you."

Raju shrugged his shoulders.

Nico paused. "Every moment's an opportunity," he said, as though knowing better than to question Raju directly.

"Yes, I suppose it is." Raju nodded, feeling flattered that such an important man was sitting beside him on his tree trunk.

"Right now," said Nico. "This moment's an opportunity."

"What for?"

Nico nodded his head slowly, stroking his small goatee beard, apparently pleased that he had got Raju's attention. "Well, for you to ask me questions. I have a few minutes while my boys pack up the crayfish."

"Questions?" Raju was puzzled. "What about?"

It was Nico's turn to shrug his shoulders. "Up to you. Life? Is everything all right with you?'

"Yes." Raju frowned. "Why shouldn't it be?"

"You don't have a job, do you? Why don't you come and work with me?"

"I don't know anything about food and beverage," he said with a laugh.

"You can learn. You have a natural talent for pleasing people, I know that. I've watched you for months. Why else do you think

138

I allowed you into the hotel to dine with our guests?"

"Ah!" Raju understood. It was fitting into place. *What happens, happens.* "Could you teach me about caring for guests, about wines and food?"

"Yes." Nico carefully stubbed out his cigarette on the heel of his shoe. "If that's what you would like."

"Tell me," said Raju, seizing the opportunity. "The last woman I dined with at the hotel kept on asking me questions, as though testing me. For instance, she asked whether I wanted Chardonnay or Shiraz with the fish." Raju looked challengingly at Nico. "What did she mean?"

Nico smiled, his eyes glinting wickedly. "What did you tell her?"

"I said I don't drink."

"Smart!" Nico clapped Raju on his knee in a fatherly way. "Join me and I'll teach you about wines, about dishes, about menus, about conducting yourself in a manner that pleases people. And how to look after them."

"I thought I did that already." Raju sighed. "But I'm not a plaything."

"Of course you're not. You're an asset. You look good, you *are* good. I can teach you how to add to that with knowledge so you earn respect." He leaned over, speaking softly as though sharing a secret, and said directly into Raju's ear, his beard scratching Raju's cheek, "As well as earn money."

#

Raju's initiation into the world of hedonism, of knowledge beyond his village existence, added finesse to his natural talent of being obliging. Under Nico's instruction he learned the etiquette, not just of wining and dining, but of gracious manners, how to compliment people, make them feel good. Already a patient listener, he discovered how to acquire information and broaden his knowledge so he could sustain conversations on what interested people.

He copied Nico in style and dress, always looking respectable so he could go anywhere whenever invited. He didn't grow a goatee like Nico but shaved every morning, massaging his face with moisturiser to keep his skin glowing and radiating youth. He looked sensational, attracting glances whenever he walked through the hotel's restaurant with Nico whispering into his ear about each of the guests, before greeting each one by name.

"Remembering a person's name and what they like to eat or drink will make them feel special," said Nico. "And they are special, always bear that in mind, even the woman who only orders coffee. She might be the most special of them all."

What Nico told him about dealing with people, Raju knew instinctively. It was the niceties the manager added, like telling him never to use his mobile phone when in company. "Always turn it off when you are with someone," he said. "That person is special, not those invisible contacts who aren't with you."

Nico explained how to order from a menu when someone else is paying. "Look at the prices quickly. Never choose the most expensive item as the person who's invited you will suspect you of exploitation. Don't choose the cheapest either, as that indicates you think the person can't afford more. Go for the middle range."

Raju realised that Nico was teaching him how to be cunning, not just how to be liked. When Nico put him to work as a steward in the restaurant, he learned how to set up a table, which cutlery to use for each dish, and how to serve correctly. When guests asked him what dish he recommended, they ordered it because he seemed sincere and that inspired their trust. Nico grinned with pleasure and the executive chef was happy too, as the dishes Raju was told to recommend sold quickly.

Nico taught him about wines; how to open a bottle deftly with a French corkscrew, and how to pour with a slight twist so not a drop of wine was spilled. He memorised the names and origins of different wines, and conversed confidently about them when asked his advice by a diner. He served behind the bar making classic cocktails with style. "Never deviate from the cocktail recipe," Nico instructed. "A Pisco Sour, a Margarita, a Negroni, should always taste the same wherever it is served."

The bar takings soared when Raju was the bar tender. "Perhaps it's because you don't drink, so you don't sample the stock," Nico told Raju. "But I think it's you. You attract customers, they like to talk to you. They order another drink because of you."

Raju smiled his appreciation at the compliment but said nothing. He was giving pleasure even though he was acting and felt he had lost his soul. As Nico's disciple, he was what the strange man had promised: an asset.

One afternoon, Nico called him to his office. There was an immaculately dressed woman with spiky, flame-red hair sitting beside Nico's desk. With a sweep of his eyes, which the woman surely noticed because of his long eye lashes, Raju formed an instant impression of her. He recognised her as being like those who had used him when he was innocent and too eager to please. He looked at Nico for guidance and saw the man's smile, which he had always seen as encouraging and benevolent, was transformed, his teeth bared in a rictus of evil.

He stifled his urge to escape from the office, bowing his head politely as Nico introduced the women. When she extended a hand heavy with rings, he raised it to is lips and kissed it briefly.

141

He looked directly into her eyes, as he had learned from Nico he should always do when being introduced to a woman. "It's a pleasure to meet you," he said, adding "princess" to flatter her.

"Yes," said the woman to Nico, ignoring him. "He'll do."

Nico stroked his beard to a point, grinning with a meaning that Raju didn't understand. "Madam has a job for you. She is opening a new night club in the capital."

"It's called Lucifer's," the woman interrupted with a sly smile. "I need you to come there as manager and host, to use your knowledge, charm and special talent to make it popular. Nico says he has trained you himself so that means you are perfect for me."

Raju looked in desperation at Nico who stared back at him sternly. "This is the moment, Raju."

"I'll be happy to be of service, madam." Raju said, even as he knew he didn't mean it.

"That's settled then," the woman said, standing up to leave.

Raju reached for the door and held it open for her.

"You will be my permanent escort, you will accompany me to society functions to publicise Lucifer's. You will stay with me in the penthouse of my apartment block. Lucifer's is in the basement." As she swept out of the office, leaving behind the scent of an expensive perfume with a whiff of charred cinnamon, she said over her shoulder, "Nico will make all the arrangements and explain the details."

Raju saw his past catching up with him. *What happens, happens.* He sighed.

Nico nodded his head. "Don't worry, son. Because of all I've taught you, and your natural ability, you can cope with even the devil herself."

13. A Perfect Match

Kathy was weeding the herbaceous border in her front garden when she heard the bell of the postman's bicycle as he rode up to the gate.

"Another three for you today, my dear," he announced, handing her the envelopes. "The same as the others you've had recently. Ten in all, I think, my dear, and all from London."

"Thank you, Joe," she replied, tucking her mail firmly into the waist band of her gardening jeans.

"Got friends in London, have you?"

"Oh, hundreds." She smiled, thinking, *And that's all the information you're getting out of me, my man!*

Joe adjusted his delivery sack onto his shoulder and, raising his hand in salute, pedalled off to resume his deliveries. "By the way, my dear," he called over his shoulder, "Mrs Brown has had a postcard from her sister in Eastbourne. The expected baby was a boy, eight pounds, three ounces."

"Goodbye, Joe," Kathy shouted after him.

"And a brown envelope from the hospital for Miss Simms," he added, as he swerved to avoid Mr Lucas's cat. "It's probably her results." The postman disappeared from view, and Kathy took her letters into the kitchen to read them.

Joe had been correct in his calculations. Ten identical envelopes had been delivered to Kathy, in twos and threes, over the past few weeks. And now Kathy spread the contents of each out onto the kitchen table. She poured herself a coffee, lit a cigarette and studied them in minute detail.

It had been the fault of her friend Margery. *Well*, thought Kathy, civilly. *Not so much a fault as an idea.*

They had been finishing a bottle of claret after enjoying their weekly 'Ladies Who Lunch' date, when Margery had suddenly asked, "How old are you, dear?"

Kathy, more than a bit put out and rather annoyed replied, "I'm thirty-nine, the same as you!"

"Well," her friend had said. "Please don't take offence, love, but you look over fifty."

Kathy had put her glass down on the table and rose with as much dignity as she could muster. "Goodbye, Margery," she said. "I must go and collect my pension. Thank you for lunch."

"Oh, *do* sit down, you silly goose." Margery laughed. "I am your best friend—known you since primary school, so I think I'm allowed to make a few friendly comments. Now," she continued, "when did you last go to the hairdresser? When did you last weigh yourself? When did you last go out and have a good time?"

Kathy sat down again. "I'm in a rut, aren't I?"

"Somewhat."

As the two best mates sat opposite each other at the restaurant table, Kathy not only took Margery's advice, but also the address that her friend handed to her. Kathy was embarking on an adventure. She was going to join an Introduction Agency.

Pros and Cons, she thought, as she gazed at the photographs of the ten men who had sent her their profiles. Percy, she discarded on the grounds that she hated the name Percy. Thomas and Douglas were also put to one side, because, although they were probably both extremely nice chaps, they had moustaches, which Kathy couldn't abide.

After another read through of the remaining seven, John was added to the pile for the waste bin, as he lived nearly 30 miles away, and Louis, although terribly good looking, was a non-driver, and Kathy had stipulated in her profile that the Agency had sent to the ten hopefuls, that she would drive half the way to a suitable venue to meet a date.

And as Vic was apparently looking for a 'tactile' lady, Kathy, having looked the word up in the dictionary, decided she would have to work a bit harder to reach that particular requirement.

After the six rejects had been binned, Kathy studied the four remaining hopefuls. *Yes,* she thought, *four is a good number to start with.* And, putting them into alphabetical order, she telephoned and made dates for the following week with Eric, Ken, Ralph and Tony.

#

"Are you gay, Uncle Mike?"

"What?" Michael Scrivener looked up from his deckchair on the beach and stared at his twelve-year-old nephew. He was babysitting the boy while his parents took a bus into town, to buy supplies for their rented self-catering cottage by the sea.

"I just wondered," said the boy, digging his toes into the sand. "I mean I don't have an aunty, so I thought you might be gay."

"Where on earth did you get that idea, Keith?"

"I don't mind if you are gay, Uncle. Lots of people are, you know."

"Are they?" Michael frowned at the boy. "Who told you that?"

"It's human nature, I believe. Some men only like other men.

145

They're gay."

"Well, I'm not," said Michael with a shudder.

"So why don't I have an aunty?"

"Because your aunty, my wife, died before you were born, young chap."

"Oh yes, I remember Mummy saying so. I'm sorry."

"For my wife dying?"

"No. For me thinking you are gay."

"Keith," said Michael, reaching over to pat the boy on his shoulder. "You mustn't think that just because a man isn't married, he's gay. He might have girlfriends."

"But you don't."

"How do you know? I could have a secret girlfriend your mummy doesn't know about. I don't tell my sister everything."

Keith paused to think about that, while Michael decided he had been sitting in the sun for too long. "Let's go and get some ice cream," he said, standing up and shaking the sand off his trousers. He was not used to spending time on the beach and Keith's odd question bothered him.

Julie, the love of his life, had died in a horrendous car accident when she was pregnant. He had married her when he was twenty and they had two marvellous, happy years together. He was so distraught, he vowed never to marry again as he wanted to keep the memory of Julie as his wife for ever. After twenty years as a widower, he had grown used to living alone, dating occasionally, and occupying himself with his career as a dedicated dentist. He enjoyed his life and thought he was comfortable with it.

It had never occurred to him that people might think, because he wasn't married, that he was gay. *Whatever do they teach children at school these days?* he wondered, as he watched Keith happily enjoying the ice cream.

"Do you want an aunty?" he suddenly asked the boy.

Keith looked up at him and smiled. "That would be nice," he said. "For you, Uncle Mike, not for me, although it would be super to be a complete family, wouldn't it?"

"Yes, I suppose it would."

"All my friends have aunties. They give them hugs, and spoil them rotten." Keith sounded as though repeating something he'd been told. "Uncles don't do that. They are kind and considerate like you and give advice."

"And you'd prefer to be spoiled rotten by an aunty?"

"Wouldn't you, Uncle Mike?"

He chuckled. "Yes, I suppose I would."

When he returned to his home after the holiday with his sister, her husband and Keith, he thought about what his nephew had said. He decided that perhaps he had been alone too long and needed a wife, the aunty Keith thought he should have. As a dentist, he was used to standard procedure, not chance opportunity. He decided to go about finding a companion scientifically, leaving nothing to chance. He signed up with an introduction agency.

#

Kathy awoke with a fluttery feeling in her stomach and a rather fast heart-beat. She had spent a disturbed night, and felt a bit washed out and insipid. Gosh, she was going out with a man for a luncheon date—a man she had never met before, but had only spoken to on the phone. *I haven't dated anyone for, goodness me,* she thought, *about twenty years.*

In the bathroom, she stared at her reflection in the mirror.

Margery was right, she looked a bit of a mess. And the photograph that had accompanied the details sent by the agency of Eric, whom she would be shaking hands with in a few hours, had shown such a good-looking chap.

Kathy showered and rollered her hair. Her outfit for the occasion was already hanging on the wardrobe door; a pretty pink cotton suit teamed with a lacy white blouse, and white stilettoes, which she hoped would see her through her date without pitching her forwards into either her meal or the lap of Eric. They had arranged to meet at midday, at a quiet little pub which they discovered was ten miles away from each of them.

At eleven o'clock Kathy opened the garage door to greet her little Fiat which would take them on the biggest adventure she'd had for simply ages.

"Where are you off to, dear?" came the voice of Nancy, her neighbour.

"Oh, there's an exhibition of quilting in Summerstown," replied Kathy. "I thought I'd see what it is all about."

"You look very smart, dear," said Nancy.

Kathy thought she heard an edge of suspicion in the comment. "See you later," she called, and drove off.

Eric was late. Four minutes, then five and then six minutes late. Kathy felt as though the eyes of everyone at the bar or around the tables in the pub were fixed on her. But suddenly she felt a hand on her shoulder, a wonderful bunch of anemones placed in her lap, and a charming voice saying, "You must be Kathy. I'm so sorry, my dear, there was a shed load of chickens on the bypass."

She smiled at her date. He was extremely smart, dapper almost. A cravat, for heaven's sake. No denying he was a nice-looking man. But she decided that Eric must also have a nice-looking son, because the photograph she had received was that of a chap a good thirty years younger than Eric. He surely must have borrowed a picture of his son!

They had a wonderful meal, and Eric told Kathy all about himself. *All* about himself. On and on and on and on. She'd had a glass of wine whilst awaiting his arrival, and another with her steak, and she felt sleepy and a bit worried about driving home. She made her excuses and said she would have to go.

He got a bit uppity and asked if they could meet again, because he thought she was, "a fine filly."

She almost neighed in reply but, kissing him on the cheek said, "We'll see, Eric, and thank you for the meal," and departed the pub at speed.

Driving home she thought she felt a bit like a prostitute. Eric had paid for everything, she hadn't even offered to buy coffee! "*Oh well,*" she thought, "*one down and three to go. They can't all be as bad as lonely old Eric!*"

Safely home and changed from the pink suit into jeans and T-shirt, she pondered about phoning Margery. But no, her friend had no idea that Kathy had joined the Agency and was to enjoy a whole week of 'having a good time'. She would tell Margery all about it when they met on Friday for their Ladies Who Lunch meeting. Tomorrow she would wear her black frock with the poppies on, and she would drive in the opposite direction from today. Away from Eric, to the neighbouring town to meet her second date, Ken.

#

Mike was asked to look after his nephew, Keith, again. His sister knew Thursday was his day off, so she had arranged for her hair appointment for that day at lunch time. As her husband was away on a business trip and Keith was still on holiday from school, she didn't want to leave him alone at home.

Mike was pleased at the chance to get to know his precocious nephew better. He asked the boy where he wanted to go for lunch, expecting him to say Pizza Hut, Macdonald's or KFC, but he said Corfu, a restaurant in the next town.

"Marcus, he's my best friend, says the food's super but I wouldn't like it because it's Greek and I don't like Greek at school."

"Good idea," Mike said. "Because you won't know until you've tried it."

And try it he did, enjoying everything Mike ordered for him. They had finished the meal when the boy drew his attention to a woman, sitting alone at a table at the other side of the restaurant. "I think she's been stood up," he said.

"Really? Why do you think that?" Mike looked across the room to where a woman wearing a black frock with bright red poppies on it was studying the menu. He noticed how her hair had obviously been carefully brushed and groomed, as it caught the sunlight streaming through the restaurant's window. She looked about his age. *Probably a widow or divorcee,* he thought.

Keith leaned across the table and said in a whisper. "She keeps on looking at her watch. She's tapping her fingers on the table top. She's disappointed."

"How do you know that?"

"That's what Mummy does when she's tired of waiting for Daddy to meet us as arranged."

Mike smiled at Keith. "Well, Sherlock Holmes, you could be right."

"Shall I ask her to join us?" Keith cocked his head to one

side and looked at Mike, as though challenging him. "She could be the aunty we're looking for."

"Keith!"

"You'll never meet my aunty if you don't do something about it." He stood up.

"Where are you going?"

"You'll see." Keith walked boldly over to the table where the woman was sitting, gazing out of the window. "Excuse me, Miss."

The woman turned in surprise and looked at him as he stood beside the table.

"Yes?"

"Would you like to join us. That man's my uncle. He's all right," Keith said. "He's a dentist. He's not trying to pick you up."

The woman looked across the room and saw a man smiling apologetically, making a sort of "I don't know what the boy's doing" gesture. She shook her head. "No thanks," she said. "I'm waiting for my date."

"Isn't he awfully late?" said Keith. "I doubt if he's coming."

The woman looked startled.

"I hope the boy's not troubling you." Mike strode over and put his hands on Keith's shoulders. "I assure you I didn't send him to talk to you. My name's Mike," he said, holding out his hand. "Michael Scrivener. I'm a dentist."

"I told her that already," said Keith.

"I'm Kathy." She shook his hand briefly.

"Nice to meet you, Kathy. Come on, Keith, we must go."

"Aren't you going to ask her for a date?" the boy whispered.

Kathy heard what he said and stared at them both in astonishment. She liked the look of Mike in his well-cut suit and beautifully manicured hands. His confident courtesy put her at ease. She laughed and shook her head. "I think I've had enough of dating," she said.

Again, Mike gave that look of helplessness at Keith's behaviour, as he steered the boy away from the table.

"His clinic is in the next town," said Keith over his shoulder. "He's not married and he's not gay. I'm sure he likes you."

Kathy watched them leave, wondering what had just happened. Her date. Ken, obviously wasn't coming so that was another off the list. "But the dentist is rather nice," she thought.

Kathy drove home, her head in a whirl. Had she just been chatted up? Surely not, he was just being polite and apologising for the comments of that cheeky young boy. She decided that she had been 'flattered.' Gradually her mood of slight euphoria gave way to one of anger. She'd been stood up! *How dare he!* How utterly humiliating, and so obvious that even a complete stranger, that divine dentist, had noticed.

Returning home, she left the car in the driveway. She had another date that evening, with Ralph. Two dates in one day, what a hussy she was becoming. She only hoped that the meal they would order would be ample, as the lunch with Ken had not been forthcoming, and she was hungry.

"You look nice, dear," came the voice of neighbour Nancy. "Been for a spin, have you?"

"That's right, Nancy," Kathy replied crossly. "And, before you ask, I'm going out again this evening to dine with an old school friend. I shall wear my pale blue skirt teamed with a darker blue gypsy-style blouse, and I see that you are cutting your hedge and have missed a bit!"

The answer phone was signalling a message received when she entered the house. A bleating voice announced that it was

Ken. "I'm so sorry, Kathleen." ("Kathy!" she shouted at the phone). "It was mother, you see. I still live at home, and if I want to meet a lady I have to, sort of, slip out. She doesn't like me to have lady friends, you see. I told her I was going to the library, and she gave me a list of the books she wanted me to get for her, and then she noticed I was wearing my best suit, and got in such a state her blood pressure shot up. So I didn't dare leave her. But I really would like to meet you. Please phone me back."

"In your dreams, Ken," replied Kathy to the machine, and erased his message forever!

#

Kathy drove the little Fiat down darkening leafy lanes and stopped, triumphantly, in the car park of a charming *olde worlde* pub. She got out and smoothed down her skirt. A smiling gentleman stood in the doorway, holding out his hand for her to shake. "You must be Kathy," he beamed. "And a pretty picture you make, my dear."

She smiled her thanks, and thought that Ralph didn't look too bad himself! Grey slacks, cream polo-neck jumper, navy blazer with some sort of badge embroidered on the pocket. He took her arm and led her into the pub.

He had booked a table for two, cosily hidden in a snug corner. A red rose was draped by her place mat. "A perfect rose for a perfect lady," gushed her date.

Oh glory, thought Kathy, *he's coming on a bit strong, isn't he?*

They studied the menus and ordered their meals. Ralph leant across the table and took hold of Kathy's hand. *Help,* she thought to herself in panic. *He's either starting with my hand and working his way up, or else he's after my gold bracelet!*

"Tell me about yourself, Kathy," he whispered in a husky voice, gazing into her eyes, and looking slightly moist at the corners of his mouth.

"Well," began Kathy, "I work from home, and…"

"Oh no, no, no, dear Kathy," said Ralph with a smirk. "Tell me about your fantasies!"

That does it! she thought. But since she was extremely hungry, she decided that she would eat the dinner Ralph was paying for, and then excuse herself, head for the ladies' lavatory and escape. She took a deep breath. "Oh," she said, "I fantasise about winning the Lottery, and what I should do with all those millions."

He dropped her hand rather crossly. "No, my dear," he said, frowning. "I mean your *real* fantasies, the naughty ones!"

Fortunately, at that moment, a waitress brought the food which saved her the trouble of replying.

"I just love to watch a woman eat," said Ralph. "I can see that I shan't be needing any Viagra with you, Kathy, dear."

Kathy lay her cutlery down on the table, gazed in regret at her untasted dinner, shoved the perfect rose onto his own plate and stalked out of the pub. On the way home she stopped at a takeaway and bought cod, chips and mushy peas, which she ate in a layby, and ruined her skirt with vinegar.

At home that night, she lay awake, wondering how on earth her best friend, Marjorie, enjoyed blind dating the men sent by an agency. She had assured Kathy she would have a 'good time.' But a good time was *not* what Kathy was experiencing. *Three down, one to go,* she thought. Tomorrow would be Tony, at a lunchtime meeting at a riverside pub the other side of town.

Nancy was in her driveway, dead-heading the roses, when Kathy left for her date the next day. Through a thin-lipped smile, the neighbour remarked, "I should take a brolly, dear, it looks like rain. *Such* a pity to spoil that pretty dress."

In the Fiat she arrived successfully at the pub and crossed the car park to the garden. She scanned the faces of the patrons who sat at the outside tables. She tried to recall the photograph of Tony the agency had sent. Blonde, floppy hair, and probably several years younger than her. Suddenly she saw someone she knew, and, to her astonishment, the man started walking over to her.

"Kathy?" he asked.

"Of *course* I'm Kathy. I always have been." She looked at the man, perplexed. "I've come to meet someone, Tony…" She gasped in horror.

"But so have I. You're Kathy! You must be my date."

"And *you* must be the husband of my friend, Bernice," said Kathy.

Later, over drinks (but not, alas, luncheon), Tony hinted that he and his wife were very broad-minded about 'things.' "We're all at it, you know," he said.

Kathy certainly did *not* know, and, mightily shaken and rather offended, she left him abruptly and drove home.

#

The next evening, Kathy and her best friend Marjorie sat in Kathy's kitchen drinking Chardonnay and eating cheese straws. Marjorie was agog and astonished as her friend related details of her adventures dating men met through the agency.

"You poor thing," she said, and suddenly went very quiet and serious, which was so unlike her. "Well, I have given that up now," she said. "In fact, I have resigned from the agency."

"What?" Kathy was surprised. "But you said it was such fun."

"It was, but now I've met him, Kathy. I've met *Mr Right*. The agency sent me his profile and we met and… well… we sort of clicked. We're seeing each other again this weekend. He's the perfect gentleman, so well dressed and courteous. Actually, he's a dentist. His name is Michael Scrivener."

"That's nice," said Kathy, keeping her surprise to herself.

After Marjorie had gone home, Kathy busied herself in making a television dinner: wedges of quiche and a bowl of green salad. She discovered a jar of pickled onions at the back of the pantry and added it to the tray with the remainder of the bottle of Chardonnay and a can of Guinness. She carried the heavy tray to the lounge, where the television was relaying a football match. She placed the tray on the coffee table, in front of the settee where Brian sat.

"Pickled Onions," he exclaimed happily. "My favourites. I suppose," he asked, "this means no kissing tonight?"

"We'll see," She smiled coyly.

"Come and sit by me, love," he said, patting the settee. "There's an old black and white movie on soon. We probably saw it together, when we were courting."

Kathy curled up on the settee beside him. *Yes*, she thought, *he is boring and predictable. And going bald. But he is Brian, my dear husband of twenty years*. She glanced sideways at him, and felt a surge of happiness, and relief. *He'll do,* she thought.

14. Finders, Keepers

Thomas, the handyman, was just giving Eliza, the scullery maid, one against the kitchen garden wall, when her cries of pleasure turned to those of alarm.

"Thomas, stop!" she cried.

"Can't," puffed Thomas.

"But look, oh my God, just look!"

Thomas adjusted himself and turned. To his horror, standing before the pair of them and gazing in sordid interest was Master Claude, eight years old and an obnoxious, abomination of a boy. He carried a huge and beautiful kite under his arm.

"What are you doing, Thomas?" he asked.

"Well," stuttered the handyman, his ardour no longer 'ard, "poor Eliza came over feeling very faint, so I've been helping her get her breath."

"That's right, Master Claude," said Eliza, stuffing her bloomers into her pinafore pocket. "But I'm feeling much better now, so I'll go back to the kitchen."

She turned her shocked face to Thomas. "Thanking you kindly, Thomas," she said, "for a-looking after me." And she turned on her heel and left them.

"I know what you were doing," remarked Claude. "I saw the milkman doing it to Eliza, and he gave me half-a-crown and an apple not to tell my father."

"Oh, you don't want to worry your father with a little thing like me helping poor Eliza when she was poorly," said Thomas. Then, to change the subject he said, "My, that's a fine kite you've got there, Master Claude. I haven't seen that one before."

"I only got it today," the boy replied. "A sort of present from Thornycroft."

"The butler?" Thomas asked in astonishment. "Why on earth should Mr Thornycroft give you a kite?"

"Because," replied the boy knowingly, "I told him I would tell my father that I saw him putting money in his pocket when he was doing the household accounts. I'd seen him doing it before, so I said that I'd seen a kite I would like."

"That's not very kind, is it?" replied Thomas, his hands itching to grasp the little monster around his neck.

"No, it's not," smiled Claude, "and I'm going to be more unkind, because if you don't give me a florin a week, I shall tell my father about you and Eliza and you'll both get the sack. Goodbye, Thomas," and off the little tyke went.

#

Claude and his mother and father sat around the dining table, being waited upon by Eliza, who seemed a little nervous.

"Oh, Albert," said his mother in a woeful voice, "Mr Lucas has given notice. Wherever shall we find another pianoforte teacher for Claude?"

"Why has he left?" asked Albert.

"He said that he found dear Claude too difficult to teach, and that there was a clash of personalities. What nonsense, Claude has a such a pleasant personality."

"Really, Felicity, that sounds odd." Turning to his son he asked, "Claude, what have you to say about this?"

Wearing a look of the utmost innocence, Claude replied, "I have no idea, Father. I think perhaps I play the piano so well that there is nothing for him to teach. "

"Oh, you darling boy, you cherub." His mother hugged him as Claude smiled to himself, thinking of that beautiful toy steam engine given to him by Mr Lucas. He had requested a nice toy, so he wouldn't tell his father that Mr Lucas was taking some of his father's collection of watercolours home in his music case.

He had also caught Mrs Wilberforce, the cook, wearing clothes from his mother's dressing room underneath her long, sensible overcoat when she went out on her night off. The outcome of that showdown was that Claude now accepted a plate containing no less than four cakes each bedtime, put secretly in his sock drawer by the terrified cook.

#

After Claude had been packed off to bed, his parents sat awhile around the fire. "I'm not sure that the boy isn't up to some mischief," mused his father.

"Oh Albert," wailed his wife. "How could you say such a horrible thing about dear little Claude? He's a good, kind, helpful boy, and everyone loves him."

"Hmm," said Albert doubtfully. Then he brightened. "Felicity, my dear, I have to go out tonight. An important meeting at my club. An annual thing, you know."

"Oh Albert," she said, in a cracked, almost tearful voice. "But you went out last night."

"I know, my pet, but after all I am the President of the blasted thing. Such a bore."

"Well," she said in a sulky tone, "don't be late."

"I'll try not to be," he promised, "but don't wait up, my dove."

In the hall, while Thornycroft helped him into his overcoat and brushed his hat, Albert felt a glow of pleasure at the delights which awaited him. Oh no, not the club. But at the little flat he had rented for a typist from his office, the delectable Mabel.

Claude was unable to sleep, perhaps because he had eaten all the cakes cook had left in his drawer for him. Cautiously, he peeped around the bedroom. He saw there was no light shining from under Nanny's door, so he guessed she must either be asleep or visiting her friend, Dolly, his mother's maid. He had often peeped through the keyhole of Dolly's room to find she and Nanny were playing some sort of game, on top of each other on Dolly's bed.

As he lay thinking about the strange things adults did to each other, he heard a crack as his mother's door opened. He scrambled out of bed, pulled down his nightshirt so it covered him, and silently opened the door of his own bedroom. He looked out to the landing and was surprised to see the light was on and his mother, wearing only her night dress, was standing in front of a window, opening and closing the curtain as though making a signal.

He watched as his mother did it six times and then turned and went quietly down the main staircase. Claude waited a few seconds and followed her, careful not to make any noise, wondering where she was going. He knew his father hadn't come home yet as he hadn't heard the car in the drive. He crouched in a corner where he couldn't be seen and saw his mother open the front door, and step outside into the night.

This was most unusual, even exciting. He decided his mother wasn't going shopping, as she didn't have her handbag. Perhaps she was going to see the horses. Sometimes they made a noise at night and she went out to quieten them, but that was when the groom wasn't on duty and Claude had seen him that very evening.

He opened the front door and peered out into the moonlight. He saw a shadow crossing the lawn, heading for the potting shed. When the shadow, which was obviously his mother, disappeared, he waited. When she didn't reappear, he crept swiftly across the lawn, feeling the grass cold on his bare feet, and stepped without making a noise, on to the small, wooden-floored veranda of the potting shed. There was a faint light from a lantern flickering through the window. He stood on tiptoe, and peered in.

He was surprised to see the under gardener lying face up on the floor, under his mother. She was bumping up and down as though riding a horse. He wondered if the poor chap had fainted, and his mother was trying to revive him. He decided that he should tell his father the next day about how kind his mother had been, going out at night to help the young gardener. Or was it supposed to be a secret?

Claude was confused. Whenever he saw people doing strange things, they always asked him not to tell his father. And they gave him presents. He had so many secrets to keep, he couldn't remember them all. But he liked the presents. Perhaps his mother would give him a present too?

He walked slowly back to the house, let himself in through the unlatched door, silently climbed the stairs, leaving wet and muddy footprints on the carpet, and climbed back into bed, not noticing how muddy he had made the sheets.

The sound of Eliza rattling pots and pans in the kitchen below Claude's bedroom woke him. He stretched and smiled to himself, recalling the strange scene he had witnessed the night before. Of course, he was only eight years old and not fully comprehensive of the acts between his mother and Philip, the under gardener, and Nanny and Dolly, but he was sure that the little snippets of knowledge he had acquired would be put to good use. He felt all-powerful, the King of the Castle.

He was already blackmailing Dolly into giving him a large bag of gobstoppers each week, after she had discovered a dead rat, he'd put in her bed and had called him a nasty little worm who would one day come to harm. The threat of Claude telling his father what she had called him warranted her making a weekly visit to the local sweet shop. He couldn't blackmail Nanny, not ever, the simple reason being that Nanny was the only person Claude was afraid of.

Claude looked at his new wrist watch, which he kept hidden in a box of marbles under the bed and which had been a gift from Basden, the chauffeur, when the boy had caught him urinating over the runner beans in the kitchen garden. It was now six o'clock. Smoothing down his night shirt, Claude made his way silently downstairs, passing his father's study on the way. It was a strange, dark room, and one that Claude didn't like very much, but on impulse he decided to pay it a visit. Father's desk was in a bit of a mess, and, underneath the thick sheets of blotting paper there was a letter which Claude read slowly, digested, and savoured.

#

Claude regarded his parents as they sat having breakfast. Addressing Albert, he suddenly said, "Father, I would rather like to have a pony."

"I'm sure you would," was the reply. "But you're not having

one, my boy."

"Well," retorted Claude, "I think I *shall* have one after all. I shall have a little mare, and I shall call her Mabel."

Albert dropped his fork into his plate of kidneys and turned ashen white.

"No, Claude," said his mother, "you cannot ride. You haven't had any lessons."

"Oh Mummy," he said, "I am sure *you* can show me how to ride. After all, I saw you riding the under gardener last night."

Felicity fainted into the marmalade dish, and, in knowing satisfaction Claude closed his eyes, muttered a quick thank you to the Lord for the food just received, and left the room.

#

Later, a very subdued Albert and Felicity faced each other across the table, a decanter of sherry between them. They had 'opened their hearts', 'aired their differences', and admitted their peccadillos. They were ashamed, mortified and forgiving for the sake of their reputations.

At that moment Nanny came rushing into the room without knocking, followed by a flustered butler. "Oh, Madam, Sir," she cried, and collapsed into the chair that Thornycroft quickly placed under her backside just in time.

"Why, whatever is the matter, Nanny?" cried Felicity.

"Brandy, Thornycroft?" demanded Albert.

"Oh Madam," sobbed Nanny again. "He's gorn."

"Gorn... er... gone?" asked Albert, perplexed.

"The boy, sir. Master Claude. Oh my, oh my, oh my!" Sensing hysterics were imminent, Thornycroft poured a glass of water from the carafe and threw it into Nanny's face. She laughed, coughed and spluttered all at the same time, then pulled herself together and explained.

"We were on the beach flying his new kite and it fell into the trees. He ran into the wood to retrieve it - but didn't come back. The kite was in the branches of a tree, but Claude wasn't there."

Felicity started making noises to herald hysterics, caught her husband's frown and changed her mind.

"But Nanny, didn't you see where Claude went?" Albert asked.

"No, master, sir," she replied. "He just disappeared into thin air. I looked high and low, and so did the gamekeeper and some of the staff, but there was no sign of him. Oh Sir," she cried, "we must summon the police!"

A thoughtful Albert said, "No Nanny, not at the moment. The young scamp will turn up when he's hungry, but tell Cook that on no condition is she to give him any supper."

But Claude did not turn up for supper. Nor did he turn up when it was his bedtime. And in the morning, there was still no sign of Claude.

After Albert called the police, and the two officers who came had noted Claude's description had left, he decided to conduct his own enquiries, mainly because his wife was already criticising him for taking no action.

"You should have called the police yesterday, as soon we knew Claude had disappeared," she said. "You obviously don't care one bit about the boy."

"On the contrary, my dear, I do. After all it was Claude who saw you riding the under gardener and spilled the beans about that. So you now have nothing to say if I take an occasional dip in the typing pool."

"Oh, Albert, this is no time for a joke. Darling Claude has

gone."

"I'll wager he's not far away," said Albert. "I'm sure the scamp is only trying to frighten us so we'll forgive him for everything."

"Why, what's he done?"

"That's what I'm going to find out, Felicity, Nanny says the boy's sheets were muddy, as though he'd been out when he should have been sleeping. And she found half a cake in the boy's sock drawer, and a cache of gobstoppers. And a brand-new watch. Why were you spoiling him with such things?"

"That's the first I know about that," said Felicity, suddenly fearful about what her precious Claude might have been doing.

"And where did he get that kite he was flying on the beach, when he disappeared?"

Felicity gasped, shaking her head. "I don't know."

Albert soon found out, by interviewing each of the staff in turn in his study He didn't get much out of the housekeeping staff, who all seemed a bit shifty, as though protecting each other. It was Thomas, the part-time handyman who hoped to become full-time, who said Claude told him that Thornycroft had given him the kite.

"Why should he do that?" asked Albert in surprise.

"Young master said it was because he had caught Thornycroft pilfering the housekeeping money and he said he would tell you."

"Well, well, well," said Albert. "So Thornycroft bought his silence with that kite." Albert dismissed the handyman and stroked his chin thoughtfully. Gradually, he realised all the other presents the boy had collected must have been given to him for the same reason—so he wouldn't tell anyone what he had seen.

Albert chuckled. In a way, he admired the boy's gumption in

turning what he had discovered into profit. But then his heart almost stopped with fright, as he suddenly wondered if the boy had been abducted, even harmed, because of what he had discovered. Perhaps he wasn't just trying to avoid punishment or win sympathy by running away?

What if he was really in trouble? Even worse, what if the police found Claude and the boy told them all he knew about the goings-on at the Manor? The scandal would make him the laughing stock of the county. He would even have to resign from the club.

Albert was half expecting the ransom note to appear at any time and it arrived, carried by Thornycroft, on a silver tray at lunchtime. Felicity was there and they read the hand written message together.

IF YOU WANT TO SEE THE BOY ALIVE, LEAVE £200 IN THE HOLE AT THE BASE OF THE DEAD OAK BY THE EDGE OF THE BRIDLE PATH. HERE IS A LOCK OF HIS HAIR.

Felicity gave a little scream when the curl of ginger hair fell from the envelope and onto the floor. Albert looked grim and called Thornycroft. "I want every member of my staff assembled in the hall," he demanded of the butler. "Every last one of them! *Now!*"

As a bewildered and rather frightened household formed a semi-circle in the panelled hall, Albert addressed them. "None of you are in any sort of trouble," he said. "I shall ask you all to do just one thing, and you don't have to speak. Now," he continued, "If my son has been blackmailing you, will you please raise your hand."

The miserable gathering looked at each other and lowered their heads.

"Come, come," snapped Albert. "Let me be the first one to start it all off." He raised his hand and his staff gasped in united astonishment.

"Yes," said Albert, "the blighter was trying to blackmail me." He turned to his wife. "Come on, my dear, raise your hand, even *you* weren't exempt."

Felicity slowly raised a quivering arm. Gradually, the raised arms of Dolly, Thornycroft, Philip, Thomas, and Mrs Wilberforce joined hers.

"Mr Lucas, the piano tutor was being got at," said Thomas.

"And goodness knows who else," said Albert, grimly. He looked around at the raised hands and remarked, "But there is someone missing." He ordered his staff back to their duties and said to his wife, "Felicity, my dear, I think I have solved this mystery."

"Will you be bringing him back?" asked his wife, feeling overwhelmed by the turn of events. "Oh dear, I really don't like Claude very much now, do you?"

"He's an absolute horror," replied Albert.

#

Albert made his way down the lane which led to the bridle path. He knew the old, dead oak that the letter writer had mentioned, but walked past it, over two fields, until he came to a tiny cottage nestling by the side of the estate's brook. He didn't knock at the door but pushed it open, and found he was face to face with his senior gardener sitting at a table.

"Well, Phipps!" Albert said sternly. "What have you to say for yourself?"

"Oh, sir," stammered the old man. "How did you know it

was me?"

"Never mind that now," snapped Albert. "Where is my son?"

"In the back with the wife, sir, a-playing with some kittens. He's all right, sir. Quite happy really."

"Was he blackmailing you?" Albert asked, more kindly.

"Yes, sir," replied the old man, hanging his head in shame. "He caught me in the greenhouse, drinking a bottle of wine what he saw me take from your cellar. He said I should give him half my wages each month otherwise he'd tell you and you'd sack me."

To the gardener's astonishment, Albert threw his head back and roared with laughter. "Oh, you silly old chap," he spluttered. "Did you think I wasn't aware that my wine stock was diminishing? You must have consumed half of that ghastly stuff which my father left."

He lay a wad of notes on the table. "You wanted two hundred pounds," he said.

Phipps stared in astonishment at the pile of money. "Oh sir, I really couldn't take it now, really I didn't mean it. I don't know what came over me. I couldn't afford to give the boy half my wages as I was saving to buy a small place for me and the wife. I meant no harm, sir."

"Count the money," Albert said. "You'll find it's enough to enable you to move far away from here and stay away."

In bewilderment the old gardener spread the money over the table, more money than he had ever seen in his life.

"Don't say anything, Phipps, just start packing up right away, and good luck to you."

"I'll get the boy," said Phipps, unable to believe his luck. His scheme had worked even better than he expected. He rose, and went towards the kitchen door.

"No, Phipps," said Albert. "It's all right, we don't want him back."

"Don't want him?" gasped the astonished man. "But sir, you have just found him."

"No Phipps," replied Albert, "*You* found him. Don't forget that old proverb, *finders, keepers*." He winked at Phipps, walked out of the cottage and whistled his way back to the manor.

15. Trunk Call

"Have you finished?" Angela was hungry, ready to start eating, tempted by the sight and smell of the two halves of a lobster drowning in garlic butter on her plate.

"No," said her husband, Charles. "Put that fork back on the table." He leaned across and moved her glass of chardonnay about three inches away from the plate as she was about to reach for it. He held his smart phone above her plate; there was a flash from its camera. He looked at the screen. "Just one more," he said, taking another photograph. "Now I'll put that on Facebook."

"Must you?" she said. "Why did you bring that thing on holiday? I thought we were having a holiday for two, not us and your phone. You're always playing with it. It's not a smart phone, it's a dumb pocket dictator governing your life. I wish you'd put it away."

"But it makes it possible to have a souvenir of our seafood lunch on holiday," he said, tapping the phone again. "All our friends will see what a good time you're having and wish they were you."

"Can we eat now? It's getting cold."

"Of course." He was about to tuck into his whole barbecued fish when he paused. "Look," he said, picking up the phone and waving it at her. "It's got two '*Likes*' already."

"Charles," she said calmly, placing her knife and fork on the plate. "If you don't put that tiresome thing away, I shall tip this lobster over your head."

He laughed. "All right, my dear." He slipped the phone into the top pocket of his gaily patterned beach shirt. "We don't want to make a scene." He glanced around the crowded restaurant. It was the best one on the beach and popular with holidaymakers, who patronised it for its fresh sea food.

They ate in silence for a few minutes, both relishing the food. Charles raised his glass of wine, looked at Angela and said, "Darling, I love you."

"I love you, too," she said through a mouthful of lobster, splattering bits of food on her plate. "Oooh, I'm sorry," she said, swallowing quickly, reaching for the wine and taking a sip. "This is sooooo good."

He smiled triumphantly. The holiday was an extravagance but he felt Angela deserved it; a couple of weeks in a tropical paradise as a contrast to the mundane routine of their lives in Dorking. After eight years of marriage, they had no children, though not for want of trying. They were happy, good companions. She worked in her father's antique shop, while he commuted to his job as a solicitor in London.

"I'm glad you enjoyed it," he said, as they finished their meals and the steward refilled their glasses. By habit, his hand touched his shirt pocket.

"Oh, go on," she said. "See what the bloody thing says now."

"Only a minute," he said, taking out the phone. "Oh, guess what. Your father's commented."

"Dad? I didn't know he even had a phone."

"He didn't, until I gave him one just before we came away. To keep in touch."

"You didn't!" She suddenly felt annoyed. "Oh dear! I

suppose he'll be using it all the time in the shop now. Just like you!"

"Well, he's sent a Facebook comment. His first."

"Is he all right?" She had a moment of anxiety about having left her father to cope with the shop by himself for two weeks.

"Oh, yes. He just says "Ugh! Lobster? Does she know she's eating cockroach of the ocean?""

"Cockroach? That's what he says on that thing? He used the phone to say my delicious lobster is like a filthy cockroach? That's it!" Angela stood up quickly. "I'm going home, *now*."

"Home?" Charles stood up too and signalled to the steward for the bill. "You mean home as in *home to Dorking*?"

"No, you silly solicitor." She was close to tears. "Home to the *hotel*. I'll walk along the beach. You can stay here and play with your stupid Face-phone, or whatever you call it."

Charles stared in bewilderment as his wife made her way past the tables of happy holiday makers towards the steps at the side of the restaurant down to the beach. He noticed Sebastian, the hotel bore who had formed a one-way friendship with them on their arrival a few days earlier, put his arm out to give Angela a pat as she passed his table.

He heard him shout tipsily, "And how's the delectable Angie today? Where's the old man? Given you the elbow, ay?"

His guffawing caused those at tables nearby to stop eating and stare. Cindy, the dim-witted, simpering, bottle-blonded female who could have been Sebastian's wife but probably wasn't, giggled and said, "Oh you are a one, Sebby."

Charles, nearly choking in anger avoided the table where the ghastly couple sat and followed Angela, who was walking swiftly along the beach to the hotel. He caught up with her as she was about to enter their poolside room.

"Darling," he said, letting his concern show. "Whatever is the matter?"

Angela turned to face him. "Please, Charles," she said, brushing a strand of hair from her face. "I'm sorry. Just give me a few minutes on my own. I'll be all right, I promise. Go to the pool bar and I'll come and join you soon."

"But my love," he replied, noting that all the colour had drained from her face, "are you feeling unwell? Is there anything I can do?"

Angela gently pushed him away, and tried to smile. "Too much sun and chardonnay," she said. "I just need to lie down for half an hour, and then I'll be right as rain, you'll see. Now, off you go to the bar."

Charles stood for a while as Angela slowly closed the door to their room. He was worried and confused, but at least she didn't slam the door in his face. He reviewed in his mind the events in the restaurant to identify what could possibly have upset her as he walked through the garden to the bar beside the pool. Greatly perturbed, he hoped that a drink would help solve the mystery.

Angela arrived at the bar sooner than he expected. She had changed from the tight white shorts and tiny crop-top that she had been wearing for lunch into a very pretty sun dress. Charles smiled his approval, and reached out and took her hand.

"Are you feeling better, darling?"

"Much," she replied.

"Angela," he said, "I'm really worried about you. What on earth happened in the restaurant? Was that ghastly Sebastian making rude signs to you?"

She laughed. "Don't be silly, dear. I don't take any notice of randy old men like him. You should see the ones who come looking for antiques just to chat me up."

"Well, I'm at a complete loss to know what happened."

"It's nothing, really. But I would like a drink."

"Right," Charles replied. "Let's drop the matter. What would you like?"

"A Margarita would be nice."

They sat in silence for a while, he drinking a pink-coloured cocktail, which he said was called a Negroni, and she sipping at her ice-cold Margarita.

"Oh," she said, "I think this is making me a little tipsy."

Charles laughed. "Well, we are on holiday. We can do things we wouldn't do at home."

"Like having a cocktail *after* lunch?" Angela laughed. "It's better than spending my afternoons with a lot of old grandfather clocks and antique furniture. Come on," she said, draining her Margarita and slipping down from the bar stool. "Let's go on the beach. I want to feel the sea breeze in my hair, to feel free!"

She ran like a young girl across the grass to the beach, her laughter reassuring him that she had shaken off her moodiness. He signed the bill for the drinks and walked quickly over to join her where she was waiting by a fishing boat hauled up on the sand. She looked beautiful at that moment, the sun making her hair shine, her beach dress hugging her slender frame as the breeze billowed across the sand.

"I ought to take your photo," he said, reaching for his phone. Then he stopped. "If you like?"

"Sure," she said. "Holiday snaps. Go on, I'll pose." She put one hand on her hip and held her dress down in the breeze with the other. She smiled provocatively.

He sighed and put the phone back in his pocket. "Not like that." He took her hand. "Let's walk."

"I thought you liked taking photographs," she said, as they strolled hand-in-hand just clear of where the sea lapped the sand.

"I do. When it's something unusual or interesting to put on Facebook for friends to see."

"So I'm not interesting?"

He glanced at her and was happy to see she was smiling. "You're teasing me," he said. "You know I didn't mean you. It wouldn't have been a good photograph. I was shooting into the sun."

Their silence was one of contentment. Laughing together, they dodged the surf as it surged up the beach. After half an hour, they turned and walked back to the hotel. By the gate there was a notice, advertising a boat cruise on the river the next day. "Let's go on that," said Angela. "We might even see crocodiles."

They went to the hotel's lobby to sign up for the boat trip. As the receptionist took their reservation, they heard the unmistakable guffaw of the odious Sebastian.

"Ah hah!" he cried, sweat pouring off his brow, which he wiped with the back of his arm. He was a bright pink from too much sun. Cindy stood meekly beside him, clinging to his arm. "Going on a tour?"

"A boat trip," Charles said coolly, in an effort to be polite.

"Jolly dee! We can share a boat. Put us down as well," he said to the receptionist. "Room 66, clickety click."

Charles and Angela shared a look of alarm.

"Don't worry, Angie," Sebastian said. "If you fall in, I'll rescue you."

"Oooh, Sebby, you are a one! Come on," said Cindy, "let's go to the room and have a shower."

"Cor!" said Sebastian. "Right on!"

As the couple walked away from the desk, Angela gripped

Charles's hand tightly. "What are we going to do?"

Charles grinned. "I know," he said. "You go to the room. I'll fix this."

Angela did as he suggested, walking slowly through the garden to their poolside room, careful to avoid Sebastian and Cindy who were lurching along another path. Charles caught up with her as she reached the veranda of the room.

"It's all fixed," he said. "I cancelled the boat trip."

"Oh, but I wanted to go."

"Instead, we are going on a guided tour by private taxi. We leave early in the morning, so we won't even see Sebastian. We're going to an orphanage."

"No, thanks!" Angela shook her head. "We're not going to adopt a baby."

"Of course not." He chuckled at her confusion. "It's an elephant orphanage. I don't think a baby elephant would like it in Dorking." He opened the bedroom door and they stepped in together.

Angela laughed happily. "Oh Charlie," she said in a squeaky voice like Cindy, "You are a one!"

They made love with a vigour that astonished them both. Then, spent and exhausted they lay on the bed and slept. Angela was the first to make a move.

"I'm hungry," she announced.

"You're greedy," mumbled Charles, reaching for her.

"And *you're* joking," she laughed, slipping out of his grasp and making her way to the bathroom.

"What shall we do after dinner?" Charles shouted above the sound of the gushing water.

"There's a band on the beach tonight," she yelled back at him. "I think I'd like to go and see it. Maybe there will be dancing."

"Dancing?" he bawled. "We haven't danced for years! Since we were courting."

"I have," she replied, in a normal voice as she emerged from the shower and surveyed the rail of clothes hanging in the wardrobe. "I danced with a hot, sweaty, panting man at the annual Antique Collectors shindig last year. He kept grabbing my bottom."

"Lucky man," said her husband, with a chuckle. "Was he like Sebbie?"

"Oh, nowhere *near* as sweaty," she giggled in reply.

The dinner was a huge buffet meal of six different counters, loaded with salads, cold meats, baked fish and roast joints of beef and pork with crackling, and an array of vegetables, rice and pasta, as well as a dessert counter with ice cream and crepe suzettes cooked to order.

"I *must* take a photo of this," said Charles, leaving Angela to walk alone to a table while he pulled out his smart phone and took several shots of the food display. "Come on," he said, joining her at the table. "Come to the buffet counter and fill up your plate. I'll stand with you and take a selfie."

"I think you mean a 'selfish,'" she said. "We're here to eat not to amuse your Face-phone friends."

She piled her plate high with everything that took her fancy while Charles, having put his phone back in his pocket, did the same. When they returned to the table with their loaded plates and sat down, they gazed at each other and burst out laughing.

"Do you think we've overdone it?" Angela said.

Without replying, he whipped out the phone and took a quick shot of her staring at her plate.

"Charles!"

"All right. I'll put it away."

They ate in silence, trying to devour all the food. Angela glanced at Charles and ginned. "Your face is swollen up like a monkey's," she said. "Are you storing food in your cheeks?"

"Well," he retorted, "I saw you undo the top of the zip on your skirt." They smiled into each other's eyes.

"You don't really want to dance tonight, do you?" he asked. "Not after that massive meal, surely."

"Let's see what the band is like anyway," she said, rising slowly from her seat.

They made their way across the dining room to the foyer, aware of the stares and admiring glances as they passed the tables. *We've still got it*, Charles thought. *And my wife is the most beautiful woman in the room*. To him, Angela looked fantastic, in her floor-length skirt, swirly and black with gold sequins. The crisp white top she wore just off-shoulder, showed a tantalising half-moon of her wonderful bosom. Her hair, which was long and usually rolled into a bun at the back of her neck, tonight was thickly plaited and hung halfway to her waist.

Charles knew, from the winks and pouts and knowing looks from the women who paused in their eating to glance at him, that he was looking good too. Trim figure in pale blue slacks and snowy white shirt, open two buttons from the neck, revealing his suntan.

A wooden dancefloor had been laid out on the beach. The band was great fun, playing pop songs from the past, that all the guests, whatever their nationality, seemed to know. Dancing was not an option—it was a must! Angela and Charles joined the throng, kicked their heels, swivelled their hips and raised their arms along with the rest of them.

Suddenly Angela grasped Charles's arm in horror. "Oh my

gosh," she cried. "There's Sebastian and Cindy. Heavens above, what *do* they look like?"

Cindy was half wearing a white leather micro miniskirt, which had risen almost to her crotch. A patch of black knickers showed as she raised her arms and wriggled her butt. Sebastian looked like an enormous melting candle. He wore palm tree patterned beach shorts, with a pair of printed coconuts in a strategic place. He was, alas, topless. His belly hung below his waist. It was not a pretty sight.

"Oh dear," said Charles. "They're coming over!"

Sebastian drunkenly saluted them, almost falling over in the process. "Take a photo," he said. "Of me and Cindy."

"What?"

"Yes, you've got your camera phone, haven't you? Saw you using it at the buffet."

Avoiding Angela's glare of disapproval, he quickly took out his phone and snapped Sebastian with Cindy wrapped around him.

"Thanks, mate. Put it on Facebook: 'Seb and Cindy at the Palais de Danse' so I can see it when I sober up!"

At that moment the band, as if on cue, began playing a slow number and Charles, catching hold of his wife, smiled at Sebastian and said, "Sorry, old boy. This is a favourite of ours," and waltzed Angela away.

Angela followed Charles immaculately, leaning in close to him, aware of how people were admiring the way they danced so well together, just as they used to when courting. She whispered quietly in his ear between teeth clenched in anger, but smiling all the time, so nobody knew what she was saying.

"If I see you use that bloody selfish Face-phone again when you're on holiday with me, Charles, I shall go home, and I do mean to Dorking!"

#

"Good morning, sir, madam. I am your driver guide for visit Elephant Orphanage. My name Joe."

Angela and Charles blinked in the sunlight as they emerged from the hotel, and were confronted by a middle-aged man holding a car door and beckoning them to get in. They did so obediently, Angela uttering a small groan as she sat down.

Joe, sitting behind the wheel of the car, beamed at her. "Long drive," he said. "Two hours. Relax."

"Oh, I will," she said sleepily, leaning her head against Charles's shoulder.

"Don't you want to watch the scenery?" he said.

"No, a little rest. Too much wine and dancing last night."

He laughed. "Yeah, I feel rough too."

They dozed for most of the drive into the hills until Joe announced they had arrived. He steered the car to the gate of the orphanage and opened the car door for them to descend. "Here's your admission tickets," he said. "It's included in tour price."

Charles took the tickets, helped Angela from the car, and looked around him. "How do you feel?" he asked her.

"Fine," she said. "Mmm. I think I can smell elephants."

"That's elephant poo," said Joe. "It's collected and used to make special fibrous writing paper. You can buy elephant paper at souvenir shop. I show you."

"Perhaps later." Charles waved Joe away and led Angela towards the admission turnstile. They followed the signs to an enclosure, where a notice informed them that baby elephants were brought there from the jungle when they lost their mothers.

"Oh, look," said Angela. "Aren't they cute."

Two baby elephants were being herded along the trail towards them. The smallest, who reached only up to Angela's knees in height, stopped in front of her.

"Keep still," said their keeper. "Don't be frightened."

"Can I stroke her?" she asked.

The keeper nodded and Angela reached down and patted the small creature's head. "She's so sweet," she said. Slowly the elephant lifted its head and, looking into Angela's eyes, waved its tiny trunk. Angela stood rooted to the spot, wondering what to do. The keeper was grinning, so she assumed this was all right.

The elephant nuzzled Angela between her legs with its trunk, and then began to raise its trunk up her thighs and under her skirt.

"Oh, Charles," she said with a cry of amazement. "Take a photograph, please. Quickly. Dad will never believe this." She stood still not daring to look anywhere, feeling the bristles of the elephant's trunk scratching her and the cold wetness of the tip of its trunk against her flesh. "No!" she suddenly shrieked.

The keeper strode over and tapped the baby elephant on its shin so it moved away. His grin seemed to say he had enjoyed the show.

Charles put his arm around her. "Darling, are you all right?"

"Ooooh, yes," she said. "I've never been groped by an elephant before. Did you get a photograph? We must show everyone."

Charles removed his arm from her shoulder and said nothing.

She looked at him in surprise. "What's wrong?" she asked.

"No photograph," he said. "I didn't bring the dumb phone with me today. I left it in the hotel. To please you."

16. The Babymoon

"Everything has a beginning, a middle and an end," said David to his son, also called David. "Sometimes, it's difficult to know which is which."

The baby he held in his arms gurgled in agreement.

"So what are you, young David? The beginning of a wonderful family life with me and your mother, the middle of our adult lives, or the end of carefree living now we're parents?"

Baby David blew a bubble. "Joyce," David called, "I think he's pooped. Come and take him."

His wife hurried into the kitchen. "You're hopeless," she said, taking the child from his arms. "You make the tea. I'll feed him."

She took the child out of the kitchen to the bedroom, knowing David didn't like the sight or smell of her breastfeeding the baby. His baby. He had insisted on naming him David.

"I want my name perpetuated," he had said. "Nothing is permanent, not even memories. But my name, David Staples, will continue through him. He'll call his son David, too."

She had smiled and said nothing, and David the baby became.

They were both working when they had decided to get married. She was the manager of a real estate agency in her home town, and he was set for promotion to manager at the bank. They were regarded as a well matched and fortunate couple with a bright future. They had a traditional white wedding at their local church but no honeymoon, as David couldn't get time off from the bank.

It was Joyce's idea to have a babymoon when she learned she was pregnant, two years after their marriage. "It makes sense," she told David. "I have maternity leave and you can get a week off from the bank now you're more secure there."

"Babymoon?" He had shuddered. "What sort of idiotic holiday is that?

She had given him the brochure. *If there's a new addition to your family on the way, it's time for a holiday for you and your partner, before baby makes three. Stoking the flames of your love with a relaxing babymoon has real long-term relationship benefits. Transitioning to parenthood can be stressful, but dedicating a vacation to reconnecting can help you be playful with each other again.*"

"What rubbish!" he said, as he tossed the brochure back at her. "It's because I stoked the flames of love that you're having a baby."

"We get extras," she said, smiling coyly.

"What sort of extras?

"Well on this hotel's babymoon package, there is a free 60-minute couple's massage, and cooking classes for us both on how to cook baby food, and a cake." She paused as he didn't seem impressed. "And a bottle of champagne in our villa on arrival."

"That sounds more like it," he said with a laugh, warming to the idea. "But why should I want to learn how to cook baby food? That's your job."

"Don't worry, David. I'm only joking. We can't afford a babymoon anyway."

It was because of that calculated comment, at which David

predictably took umbrage, that a few weeks later they arrived at an island beach resort in the Maldives, for their babymoon. Instead of being acutely embarrassed, David actually enjoyed the five-day break. He loved the couple's massage, with Joyce and he lying side by side, and had fun at the cooking class. They dined on the beach under the stars, swam every day, and even went out to sea fishing together. For him, it was better than a honeymoon as there was nothing to prove, as they both knew each other well enough after being married for two years.

The euphoria created by the few days of babymoon in the blissful atmosphere of a tropical island, far away from the pressures of work, continued throughout Joyce's pregnancy. Both of them had enjoyed 'reconnecting' and David decided the babymoon was a much better idea than having a honeymoon. It made financial sense too, as it was a holiday for three for the price of two, but there was none of the inconvenience of travelling with a howling baby disturbing everyone else.

The 'transition to parenthood' that the leaflet had mentioned was something that had never occurred to him as being stressful. Thanks to the babymoon, and the feeling of mutual trust and support it inspired, they enjoyed the months of waiting for the baby's birth.

When David accompanied Joyce to the maternity unit for her six-month scan, they were told by the nurse that the sex of their child was evident. When she asked if they would like to know, they were both adamant that they were not to be told. As they both had two sisters each, they were convinced the baby would be a girl. In fact, they had chosen girl's names, and decided upon Harriet or Yolande. They never even considered that Joyce could be carrying a boy. They had painted the nursery pink and with wallpaper of fishes swimming in a blue lagoon; David's idea, to remind them of the babymoon.

It was only after the babymoon and when he had been promoted to manager of the bank that his wife seemed to have become somebody else, not the girl he married. She began playing on his weaknesses, manipulating him so he did what she wanted. He noticed it first when she announced she was going to give up her job to care for the baby when she was born.

"We don't want a nanny," she had said. "Now you're manager, you don't want people at the bank to think your wife has to work."

When he thought about what she said, it made sense. A nanny would be extra expense, as well as introducing a stranger into their marriage. It was fortunate Joyce had suggested it because he knew, if the idea had come from him, she would have said she wanted to continue her career.

David insisted on being present at the birth but to his shame, he had fainted, which necessitated the doctor and nurses stepping over him to attend his wife. The cry, "It's a *boy!*" was so unexpected that Joyce wondered if the midwife had made a mistake. David, being fanned from unconsciousness by a nurse with a towel, sobbed with joy.

It didn't take long after the baby was born for David to realise that Joyce had become the boss of their marriage. He saw how successful she must have been at her job selling real estate, because she was so persuasive. Just as he had agreed on the babymoon, he found he was somehow always obliged to do what she wanted. It became annoying when she insisted, they shared duties in caring for the baby.

"But I've only just come home," he protested after returning from work one day. "I need a rest, to put my feet up, have a whisky."

"So do I," Joyce told him. "I've been looking after baby David all day. He needs you. You don't want him to feel you don't care about him, do you?"

When David had left for the bank the next morning, Joyce sat the baby in his little bouncer, strapped him in, and perched him safely on the kitchen worktop where he could watch her as she cleared away the breakfast dishes. He gurgled and cooed and shuffled his baby legs so that the bouncer bobbed. She smiled at him, this little miracle that she and David had created between them. He had so many of his David's characteristics; his nose, his chin, his eyes. Even the downy fluff of hair was beginning to darken. Joyce's hair was blonde. Her eyes were almond shaped and dark brown, but his were bright blue, like periwinkles.

She addressed him, "This is your Daddy's egg cup." She held it up and his eyes grew larger in wonder at the chicken-shaped, multi-coloured crockery. "And here is the piece of toast he didn't eat. Look—*toast*." Baby David cooed.

She sighed and tossed the uneaten toast in the bin. On the worktop the baby was starting to get fractious, bouncing and banging his heels. He needed feeding. Joyce released him from his bouncer and carried him to the sun lounge, where she cradled him in her lap, unleashed her breast and baby David honed in. He stared up at her as he fed, dazzling her with his periwinkle eyes.

She found herself at that moment transported in time to the babymoon, when she and David had paddled in the translucent blue waters of the lagoon, so happy together. Baby David was just a bump then, not a living being who required constant attention. She wondered whether she would ever know such contentment again. It would be ages before they could have another holiday, and they would have to take the baby with them.

That evening, when David returned from the bank, Joyce

surprised him with a kiss on his cheek and a whisky already poured out for him.

"That's nice," said David, his heart sinking as he wondered what his wife was planning this time. "Where's David?" he asked anxiously, because she wasn't cradling him in her arms as she usually did when he came home.

"In the nursery," she said. "Sleeping. He's had a busy day, just like his father, I suppose."

"Busy? Being fed and pampered by you all day? I didn't even have time for a proper lunch."

"You poor thing," she said, sounding genuinely sympathetic. "Shall I make you a sandwich while you're waiting for dinner?"

"That's all right," he said, sipping the whisky. "I'll just go and see David."

The nursery door was ajar and he peeped in at the sleeping child.

"Don't wake him," Joyce said, standing behind him and putting her arms around his waist. "Let's share these few moments while he's asleep. We can pretend we're on our babymoon again."

"Really?" David felt his body tingling at her touch. "Are you sure?"

"Yes," she said. "I'm sure." She held his hand and tugged him playfully towards the bedroom. "There's no beach, no sea, but just us."

As he lay naked on top of the bed beside her, he recalled the time they had shared a couple's massage, one of the extras on the babymoon. It had led to a passionate night in the privacy of their beach villa in a way he had never thought possible. Now Joyce had done it again. He squeezed her hand affectionately and leaned over to kiss her. The baby began to cry.

"I'll go," he said.

"But you're naked, David!" Joyce laughed.

"He's a boy, too," said David. "He won't be shocked."

In the nursery, he gently rocked the cradle, wondering what had just happened. It was so unlike Joyce; he was a bit shocked. Baby David stopped crying and gazed up at him, and he forgot his doubts. He resolved then to do what the babymoon brochure said: he was going to reconnect, be playful again.

When he had dressed and sat down with Joyce for dinner, he quietly asked, "What's on your mind, dear?"

"Nothing," she said, sounding surprised. "Why do you ask?"

"You know, the whisky to welcome me home, David asleep in the nursery when he's usually in your arms and you've no time for me, this dinner... us. No tension. It's like we were on the babymoon again."

"But now we have the baby, David. We can't go on a holiday like that again. Besides, we can't afford it."

He looked at her and frowned. "No!" he said, noisily dropping his knife and fork on his plate. "We're not going back to the Maldives for a holiday."

"Not the Maldives. That's too far. Somewhere we can take David, where children are welcome."

"You had this all planned, didn't you?"

"It's been more than a year, David. You deserve a holiday."

He sighed. She was right, as usual.

#

The baby had grown restless during the night, his whimpers gradually accelerating into full-blown howls. Joyce, pulling her nightdress tightly around her, picked the baby up from his cot and cuddled him, clucking at him like a mother hen.

"What's up with him?" David asked in a sleepy voice.

"I think he's teething," replied Joyce.

"Already!" exclaimed David. "He's not old enough to get teeth, surely."

"Apparently, teeth can make an appearance at any time," said Joyce, remembering the handbook on baby care she had read. "I'll get him some gel from the Chemist tomorrow."

She changed his nappy, kissed his cross little face and laid baby David back in his cot. Returning to bed and curling herself around her husband's back, she hoped she would pick up on the dream she had left behind when the baby had woken her. But after a few minutes of drifting comfortably into oblivion, loud, angry yells from the cot brought both of them upright.

"Your turn," said Joyce.

"Don't be silly, dear," said David. "I've got to go to work in a few hours."

"Your turn," Joyce repeated, in the firm voice that he was beginning to know and dread.

David searched for his slippers under the bed with his feet and padded over to the cot, where he picked the baby up. Holding him so he was looking into his face, he said sternly, "Now this will not do at all, young chap. Your poor old Daddy has to go to the bank to earn some money so that Mummy can have the holiday she is hankering after."

Joyce sat bolt upright in bed for the second time that night. "I *beg* your pardon," she shouted. "What the hell do you mean by that?"

"Just telling our son a few home truths," said David, rocking the baby in his arms as he gradually went back to sleep. Gently he tucked him back into the cot.

Joyce suddenly shouted, "You said *our* son? Yes, David, he is *our* son. We shared in the manufacturing of him, we shared a few antenatal classes, and we almost shared his birth before you passed out on the delivery room floor. But *who*," she screamed, "is at home with him, nursing him, feeding him, changing him, walking him all day, while you swan off to lord it over your staff and customers at your precious bank?"

David, finally losing his temper, said cruelly, "And who wanted to stay at home and be a full-time mother, refusing to have a nanny, and who thought she knew it all because she had read the books?"

Joyce howled at him, he swore at her and she, picking up the nearest missile to hand, a tumbler of water, threw it at him. It missed and smashed with a loud noise against the door, splashing the cot with water. In the ensuing, hateful silence came the sound of gasping and sobbing from the cot and wailing like a kitten in distress.

David and Joyce stared at each other in horror, and both leapt to the side of the cot. David picked the baby up in his arms, and Joyce wept hot tears onto the infant's angry, reddened cheeks.

The next morning, breakfast was consumed in silence. Baby David seemed none the worse for his initiation into the world of adults, and took to Joyce's breast gurgling with satisfaction. David, disturbed by the sight of breast feeding in the kitchen, wiped toast crumbs from his chin, picked up his briefcase, and, bidding farewell to Joyce with a nod but no kiss, left the house.

It was a difficult day at the bank for David. He read the mail, noted the reminder about the upcoming weekend seminar for managers, and swore under his breath because he wouldn't be able to go with Joyce in her present mood. He couldn't concentrate, made silly mistakes in dictation and reduced his secretary to tears. He felt ashamed. His son had heard bad words, loud oaths, lamentable sayings, being shouted between his parents. David was worried, wondering if Joyce was, in fact, ill. He felt no sympathy towards her after what he had seen of her selfish behaviour.

Somehow the business of the bank drew to its daily close. After the last customer had left, David took the time to have a few words with his staff, to apologise for his curtness during the day. He then drove home, wondering and dreading what welcome he would receive.

"David," he called, as he unlocked the door to the house. He hung his coat on the rack and placed his briefcase on the shelf below. All was quiet. He entered the lounge, where Joyce would be feeding the baby. But nobody was there.

He looked in the kitchen: it was empty and silent. He called upstairs, and then climbed them to look in the bedrooms. Nothing. Returning to the kitchen, with panic rising in his chest, he saw the note propped by the electric toaster.

We have gone. We don't need you.

Damn! thought David. *That's all I need after such a lousy day.* He sat down to consider the situation logically. Joyce had taken baby David somewhere.

Why? He had no idea. *Is this some form of blackmail to make me do something to get her and David back?* he wondered. But he had an idea about where she had gone.

He took his phone from his jacket pocket and pressed the button for his sister-in-law's number.

"Hello, David," a voice answered.

"Joyce?" he said in surprise.

"Yes, I've been waiting for your call. I knew you'd guess I am at my sister's. She is a paediatric nurse, after all. She says

David is OK. She's going to help me with him for a while. Can you manage?"

"Sure." He tried to sound confident. "You gave me a fright."

"Good. Perhaps you'll be more considerate in future."

He didn't want to argue. "It's all right," he said. "Why don't you stay there a week? I have to go to a two-day seminar for bank managers the day after tomorrow, in Exeter. I'll stay there overnight."

After they finished talking, he called the local pizza outlet to deliver a hot garlic prawn pizza for his dinner; it would remind him of the barbecued prawns they shared on the beach during the babymoon. He took the bottle of whisky and poured himself a drink. "Well," he thought. "It seems baby David has become the solution, not the problem. I can go away."

At the management seminar, David was fascinated to see one of the participants had a bump, just like Joyce when she was pregnant. She was about Joyce's age and, since she was at the seminar for bank managers, was obviously a high-flyer. He noticed the other women and men at the seminar avoided her, as if they were ashamed to sit next to a pregnant woman. At the morning coffee break, seeing her standing by herself, he strolled over.

"Hello," he said, "I'm David Staples, manager of our Castle Street branch." He held out his hand, which she took and shook for a moment longer than necessary, obviously sizing him up. He seemed to pass the test.

"Charlotte Brodie," she said, adding, "*Miss*. The Fowley Road branch."

"Miss?" David grinned. "I can't help noticing, no one can."

"That's okay. My boyfriend got cold feet and dumped me. I shouldn't have trusted a lawyer."

David laughed, feeling at ease with her. "That's a shame," he said. "I was going to suggest you go on a babymoon. I went on one with my wife, it was wonderful. But now she's left me and taken the baby."

"Post-natal depression probably," Charlotte said. "I've heard about that." There was silence between them.

David suddenly found himself saying, "Look. After this afternoon's session, shall we have drink together? Are you staying in this hotel?"

"I'd like that. Room 68."

#

David was amazed how quickly it all happened. Gin and tonic for two, dinner with a bottle of wine, and a night in Room 68 together.

"We've saved the bank some money by sharing a room," he said the next morning.

"I was promised a bonus," Charlotte said. "I didn't expect it was you."

"You have a bonus? You should spend it on that babymoon I told you about. You'll feel great afterwards."

She looked at him quizzically. "Alone…?"

For the first time for years, David felt nervous. "I have a bonus, too. Why not… I mean… well… we could go together? We don't have to be married, and it's obvious you're pregnant." He patted her bump gently as she lay naked in bed beside him.

She smiled. "No commitment?"

David nodded his head and smiled back at her. "No commitment. Not a loan. Just a beach holiday, with extras. Your babymoon."

17. The Seventh Shelter

It was the shelter farthest along the front, beyond the last of the gift shops and ice cream parlours, and just before the beautifully manicured lawns and flower beds ended, and the straggle of dock weeds and nettles began. If one could be bothered to count, there were seven shelters in all, spaced sensibly, with views overlooking the sea.

The shelter in this story is Number Seven. Over the years the other six had been occasionally spruced up, whitewashed on the outside and their inner walls scoured, leaving just faint markings of graffiti, until a few weeks later they were re-adorned with names, threats, love hearts and diagrams of impossible male genitalia. The wooden benches inside were periodically washed down at the end of the summer season, and the floors scrubbed with an industrial broom and strong council detergent. But no such treats for shelter Number Seven.

For some reason Number Seven had been allowed to age and crumble, with never a sight of brush nor broom. The outside walls still bore the slight tinge here and there of the original blue paint, now peeling away. Inside the seats were hard concrete, unlike the other six, which had been updated with wooden benches several years before. The walls were virtually graffiti free, the so-called artists preferring the newly painted walls of shelters Number One to Six. Number Seven was not a popular choice for sitting and gazing out to sea, except for a few special people.

Florence, spreading her massive hips, settled herself with a deep sigh onto the hard concrete seat. She pulled her pack of cigarettes from her bag and lit one, screwing her eyes up against the smoke and coughing her first fag wake-up call. She stared out to the sea. Nothing to note, calm as a mill pond. *Blimey*, she thought, *it's good to get a short break away from the heat of that kitchen*. Her Bed and Breakfast establishment (Bide Awhile) was fully booked for the week, and Florence had just overseen the safe delivery to all tables of five 'Full English'; two poached eggs only ("not runny, please"); one double egg, bacon and mushroom, and two vegetarian options. She had then given instructions to her 'staff' (two school leavers, one lad doing his community service and old Betty), and had removed her pinafore, donned a cardigan and crossed the road to the seventh shelter.

As Florence coughed her way through her second cigarette of the morning, her friend Ruby, the proprietor of Happy Days Guest House arrived, panting and swearing. Easing herself onto the rock-hard seat, her opening words were the same as the ones used the day before and would be uttered for the rest of the week. Ruby was a moaner. "Bleedin' kids," she growled. "I've got four of the little blighters. One of them drew a pattern on the tablecloth with the tomato sauce bottle!"

Florence tutted obligingly but smugly, as *her* establishment rules stated 'No Children Under The Age of Fourteen'. "Whatever did you do, Rube?" she asked.

"Told the mother to keep her kid under control, only to be informed that little Beyoncé was just showing her artistic temperament, and could I please stop interfering."

"Well!" said Florence in sympathy, handing the fag packet and matches to her friend.

"And," coughed Ruby, "I've got a set of four-year-old twin boys and a bleedin' moody and hormonal teenage girl."

"Couldn't be worse, Rube," said Florence.

A silence descended whilst the two seaside landladies eased their feet from their sensible shoes, pressed their aching backs against the hard but somewhat comforting wall of the shelter, and smoked in a fog of companionship.

"Ah well," grunted Ruby, pulling herself into an upright position. "Back to the grind!"

"Oooh," puffed Florence, "give me a hand up, Rube. My legs have gone to sleep and my bum's numb." They laughed.

"Why on earth do we come to this grotty old shelter for our morning natters?" asked Florence.

"Because it's straight across the road from where we live," was the reply. "And there's nobody else comes to interfere, and it's... well... it's sort of become our second home after all these years."

The two friends took one last gasp of sea air which made them choke and, after a hug, crossed the road together, with Florence opening the gate to Bide Awhile, and Ruby dead-heading a couple of geraniums before she entered Happy Days, next door.

"See you at Bingo tonight, Flo?" she called over the hedge.

"Too right you will," replied the other. And sighing they began to plan the evening menu for their respective guests.

#

Visitors to the resort (middle-aged or elderly gents, the 'early-morning-breath-of-fresh-air' group) collected their newly purchased walking sticks from the receptacles beside the front doors of their boarding houses and, shoulders back and noses to the brine, marched along the promenade. Passing shelter Number Seven they would quicken their pace, their nostrils having been assaulted by the odour of cigarette smoke. A few yards further on, a flight of steps led down to the beach and there the strollers would pause, gazing at the wide strip of sand, pure and smooth, untouched by the sandcastles, beach towels, transistor racket and the usual paraphernalia of a seaside morning. The sea, as yet devoid of any swimmers, boat-trip crafts, speed boats, jet skis and the rest of it, stretched itself out to meet the sky on the horizon. Great lungs-full of air would be greedily sucked in, causing most of the 'fresh-air-group' to come over a bit giddy, and decide to find a seat or shelter. Hastily ignoring Number Seven, they would retrace their steps and sit awhile in Number Six.

#

But Number Seven was, in fact, inhabited. A tiny lady, dressed in a black coat and with a knitted bobble hat of the same colour, sat in the corner at the back of the shelter. Every morning, summer to winter and back again, through rain, snow, fog and broiling heat, she would sit in the same spot, staring out at the sea. Sometimes, when the tide was exceptionally high and 'No Bathing' signs were erected on the beach, she was sprayed by the angry sea as it reared up to reach the promenade. Sometimes her feet got wet. But still she came, just for ten minutes or so. Just to gaze at that sea, that sea from which her Jimmy failed to return when, after the night-long search, his fishing boat was found in splinters among the rocks further round the bay. But they didn't find Jimmy.

And so, the tiny lady came, and would continue to come, just for a few minutes, just to hope for a miracle. But after forty years, the miracle was a long time arriving! With a sigh she stood and prepared to go back to her little house in the town, but not before muttering oaths and throwing a look of utter hatred out to sea.

#

The next visitors to the seventh shelter were heard before they made their appearance. A joyful, youthful burst of laughter announced the arrival of a young couple wearing the uniform of 'kitchen helpers'. Hand-in-hand and enraptured with teenage love. Alfie (he of the community service punishment), the odd-job boy from Bide Awhile, and Kayley, the trainee school-leaver learning the ropes at Happy Days. They had met at the neighbouring dustbins outside the kitchens with just a short hedge between them, and, keeping an eye open for the respective cooks and landladies, their courtship began.

They were overjoyed to discover that they were both allowed a half-hour break from the kitchens at 11 every morning. They used those special moments in cuddling and kissing in the smelly old shelter. Alfie had carved a heart into the peeling cement of the walls, with a sharp kitchen knife he had borrowed for the operation. And today, he aimed to add their names.

Alas, he spelt Kayley with a 'C', but she was still enthralled. And to his joy (and somewhat bewildered) Alfie was allowed to place his hand *above* Kayley's knee! Thirty minutes are more like thirty seconds when you are sixteen and in love, and far too soon it was time to tear themselves away from each other, sigh, one last kiss (a good'un) and across the road to their neighbouring work places.

Hard on the heels of the departing lovers, Major Llewelyn approached the shelter. A fine specimen of manhood, with his ebony cane, his grey cavalry twill trousers, his navy blazer with the brass buttons and some sort of insignia on the pocket and the tie, the special tie. He stood for a few moments looking out to sea, and then scrutinised the down-at-heel shelter. There was something rather furtive in his manner, something 'un-Majorish'. He almost slunk into a corner seat, and hid himself behind his newspaper.

He had made his way through the back streets of the town to the line of promenade shelters, turning his head to look in shop windows when anyone passed him, and crossing and re-crossing the road. The Major, you see, was in disgrace. *Big* disgrace. He had been banned from entering the small fun-fair, banned from watching the bathers in the open-air pool, banned from the local theatre and cinema and even banned from the beach!

The Major had been a naughty boy. Complaints from ladies—that was the trouble. Groping, touching. Inappropriate conversations. He had even been banned from walking the 'touristy' end of the prom, and from sitting in any of the shelters. But he felt quite safe and secure in shelter Number Seven. No decent lady would want to spend time in that smelly old cave of a place. He had been forced to leave his lodgings after his landlady got to hear the gossip about her guest on the second floor. And now he was forced to rent a damp and tiny room in the basement of a crumbling Victorian monstrosity. And that was not the worst part, not by any means.

A young reporter from the local paper had decided to try his luck with a juicy story and had sat, gleefully, at the back of the court on the exact day when Major Llewellyn had been heavily fined, threatened with prison, put on a nasty little 'list', and banned from almost everywhere in town. And the humiliation continued. The story in the newspaper next day (greatly exaggerated, of course), had printed, in bold lettering underneath his photograph 'Mr. Percival Pratt, retired carpet salesman'. His gaffe was blown, and he was exceedingly depressed.

"Ah well," he muttered to himself, "it's almost midday." And, straightening his back, tilting his straw boater at a rakish angle and swinging his ebony cane, he made his way to the police station where he had to report to the desk Sergeant twice a day, to prove that he was "being a good boy."

#

Major Llewelyn, also known as Percival Pratt, had left his newspaper on the seat in the shelter, where it was found the next morning by Florence. Squinting through the cigarette haze, she read the headlines—and read them again.

"Whatever is the matter, Flo?" asked her friend as she arrived and made herself comfortable on the bench. "You look as though you've had bad news?"

"Read that," demanded Florence, folding the paper and handing it to Ruby.

"What, more news about that galloping Major?" She laughed.

"Oh him," sniffed the other, "he's old news, he is. But just you read that there, Rube," she said, pointing.

They read it together, the dreadful news. *The District Council has agreed to the plans for a new Public Convenience to be built along the far end of the Promenade. This will result in one of the shelters being demolished. Work is due to begin next Monday. The area will be sealed off for safety.*

"Oooh, Flo," gasped Ruby. "Do you suppose it will be *our* shelter they'll demolish?"

"Sure to be," Florence replied. "It's totally knackered and it's on the end."

After a long pause, Ruby said, "I'll really miss the old place."

"Me too," agreed Florence. "Me too."

#

The workmen moved in. Red tape surrounded Shelters Five, Six and Seven, and the area resembled a war zone. Diggers, dumpers, rollers, spades, picks. Barriers and screens were erected, trenches were dug. Bricks and wood and bags of cement were delivered, Bronzed men, topless but squeezed into tight jeans and wearing hard hats stood around, whistling and smoking.

The mayor arrived, a small crowd gathered to watch. But at tea time nothing much had happened, and people moved away to seek their meal and something more interesting to watch. The gang of workman toiled until late in the evening, when the promenade illuminations came alive. And then the noise stopped, and it was knocking-off time.

Next morning Florence and Ruby had decided to have their early morning fag break on a bench beside the yachting lake. They averted their eyes from the building site, but peeped. They stared. They laughed. They wept. They hugged each other. They did a short version of *Knees Up Mother Brown.*

Along the promenade, as far as they could see, stood Shelters

Number One, Two, Three, Four and Five. *And Seven!* Of Shelter Number Six there was no sight. Just a pile of rubble.

"Oh Flo," cried Ruby, wiping her eyes. "We've still got our shelter. It was too knackered even to be demolished!"

They laughed and laughed and lit another cigarette each.

18. Sun Everything Knows

"Hello! My name is Sun. Welcome to the beach."

Richard groaned, not even bothering to open his eyes. *Not another beach boy*, he thought, pretending he was asleep. Jane, lying on a towel on the sand beside him, was polite. She always was.

"Hello," he heard her say. "Sun? That's a nice name."

"Thank you." The boy's voice was that of a teenager. Richard wondered why his wife was talking to the fellow. Their tour guide had warned them about the beach boys, always looking for money.

"If you want something," the guide had said, "just ask me. I can arrange it. Lobster dinner on the beach, a river cruise, gems. I know a very good gem store."

Yes, Richard had thought. *And you'll get a fat commission if we buy something. Just like the beach boys.*

"Sun is part of my name, madam. Actually, my full name is Jay-sun. What's your name?"

"Jane," Richard heard his wife say. He opened his eyes and sat up.

"Oh, for goodness sake, Jane. Why are you even talking to the boy? You remember what the tour guide said."

"Those tour guides don't like us."

"What?" Richard looked at the boy. He was wearing only beach shorts with a palm tree design and sunglasses. He looked fit and neat, dark hair flopping over his forehead and ears, clean shaven, with a complexion the gold of sunshine. "I wasn't talking to you."

"Don't worry, Richard," said his wife. "He's not annoying me."

"Well, he's disturbed me!" Richard rolled over onto his stomach. "Get rid of him," he said, letting his annoyance show in the tone of his voice.

"Okay, sir. Sun goes. No issues."

"I'm sorry," said Jane. "My husband's tired after the flight. We've just arrived on the island."

"Sorry to disturb, madam Jane. Beach boy, Sun not. Fisherman I am. Look my boat."

Richard covertly peeped where the boy was pointing, to the fleet of small boats with outboard motors drawn up at the sea's edge at the other end of the beach, away from their hotel.

"Where from you are?"

"England," Jane said.

"My sister England live. A nurse she is."

Richard gave a growl like an angry elephant. Jane giggled.

Sun shrugged his shoulders, flashing a broad smile revealing a set of perfect white teeth. "I go," he said. "If you any one trouble, just say Sun you know. My beach this is." He gestured up and down the long stretch of sand.

"Thank you," said Jane. "You're very kind."

In the silence, broken only by the pitch of waves on the shore, Richard rolled over and looked up. Sun was walking away. He turned and waved, and Jane waved back.

"Why are you encouraging him?" he asked angrily. "He won't leave us alone for the whole week we're here."

"Don't be silly, Richard. There's no harm in being nice."

"Nice? To a beach boy?"

'He said he's a fisherman."

"Huh!' Richard grabbed his towel and stood up. "I've had enough sun. Both of them. Shall we go to the hotel for lunch?"

Jane was surprised but stood up to join him, gathering up her towel, the sun cream and her book and putting them in her beach bag. Richard had begun to walk towards the gate to the garden of their hotel. She looked around. Sun was standing by the sea's edge, silhouetted against the waves, watching her. He waved.

She gave a quick wave of her free hand in return, glancing behind her, hoping that Richard, who was waiting at the gate, hadn't seen.

The holiday had been the idea of Jane's mother. Popping in unexpectedly to see Jane at her home after visiting the hairdresser, she immediately became concerned about her daughter's appearance. Black circles under the eyes, which showed she wasn't sleeping, and, far worse, red eyes showed she had been weeping. Jane was losing weight, thought her mother, and she looked scrawny and unhappy.

Over a cup of coffee, the whole sorry truth had emerged. "Richard," said Jane, sniffing through her tear-stained hankie, "doesn't seem to care about me any more. He hardly ever speaks to me, makes straight for the cocktail cabinet on his return from work. He has three or four shots of whisky before bedtime, and then tosses and turns all night, muttering in his sleep. He won't tell me what's wrong."

"You both need a holiday," said sensible mother, "and I shall pay for it. I've had some dividends."

"But the twins…?" said Jane.

"Sorted," replied mother. "Half term is coming up, so book now and I shall be delighted to have the scamps for two weeks."

"I shall have to ask Richard," Jane replied, with a surge of hope in her heart.

At first, Richard was extremely non-committal about taking a holiday. But then he thought, *why not*? If ma-in-law was paying and the seven-year-old twins could be re-homed for a time, it could be just what was needed. And so, he agreed, and Jane happily started packing.

The flight was long and tiring. Jane had the middle seat next to a woman in a sari who never spoke a word, although Jane tried to converse with her. Richard had the aisle seat where he seemed happy as he had easy access to the drinks service. Jane felt miserable, but on landing things could not have been more perfect.

As the tour guide briefed them, they both watched from the windows of the coach transporting them to their hotel, enthralled by the coconut palms, banana trees, rivers and the wonderful scenery unfolding before them.

The hotel room was beyond their wildest dreams, with a balcony overlooking the sea. As Jane unpacked their cases and hung the holiday attire that could only possibly be worn abroad and not at home, she could sense that her husband was happy. They had grabbed suitable beach clothes, and eagerly made their way to the beach.

How pretty she looks, admitted Richard to himself as he gazed at his wife. *She should wear pale blue more often. And I had forgotten how long her legs are.*

But then had come Sun, spoiling everything.

Dinner in the hotel dining room that evening was magnificent. Richard, having lost his irritable mood, thought Jane looked beautiful in the tight-fitting black dress she was wearing. He had been saddened, after the difficult birth of the twins, at how her once fantastic figure had suffered, and how she had taken to wearing loose, baggy clothes. But tonight, she looked wonderful.

As they tucked into the mysterious starter, which was unknown to them but tasted spicy, Jane suddenly kicked Richard's ankle under the table and hissed, "Look! Over by the door marked Kitchen. It's Sun, with a basket of lobsters."

Richard froze, as Sun made his way to their table. He no longer wore his shiny sunglasses and was wearing a T-shirt and tight jeans.

"Sun lobster today get, madam Jane. For this hotel I fish. This one your name has."

And there, on the top of the basket was a live, flapping lobster with '*Pritty laddy*' marked on the label tied around its shell.

Richard stared at him. "Go to hell," he said. "Can't you see you're not wanted?"

To his surprise, the boy winked at him, as though they were sharing a secret. "And here," he said, putting his hand under the lobsters and withdrawing a bottle, "chilled Chardonnay is, wine for master. Compliments of hotel."

"What?" Richard eyed Sun suspiciously.

"Don't worry, master. Every couple here staying on same holiday package like you, this welcome gets, lobster and wine."

"Oh well, then," said Richard, reaching for the bottle. "If it's included."

"Thank you, Sun. You're very sweet." Jane hoped he didn't think Richard was discourteous.

The boy nodded his head, flashed his brilliant smile at both of them, and sauntered back to the kitchen.

Richard shook his head. "Does he work here?" he asked,

puzzled, but Jane shrugged her shoulders. He unscrewed the bottle top and poured some wine into her glass with a larger measure for himself.

That night, whether it was the wine, the beauty of the island, or a possessive reaction to Sun's obvious interest in Jane, he made love to her with a touch of his old passion.

The next morning at breakfast, to which they helped themselves from the buffet counter, Richard looked around the restaurant for Sun. Jane noticed his agitation.

"Don't worry," she said, reaching across the table to touch his hand. "He's not here."

"Who?" he asked in surprise that she had noticed.

"Sun," she said. "He's gone fishing."

'He has? How do you know?"

"I asked at reception about him. He's the hotel's animator. He looks after all the guests, takes them fishing, snorkelling, arranges tours, dee-jays at the disco in the evenings."

"Does he?" Richard seemed to brighten. "So he's here every day, then?"

"Yes, but he won't be a pest, I'm sure."

They spent that day lying in the sun on the beach. Several times, Richard glanced towards the boats pulled up on the sand. Jane smiled to herself when she noticed, wondering if he was jealous just because Sun had spoken to her.

They saw Sun again that evening when he stopped by their table in the bar.

"Everything okey-dokey is?" he said in his funny way of speaking English. "Sun today out."

"What?"

"He means he went out today," said Jane.

"Oh." Richard gave his usual casual response.

"Sun today guests to see old fort took," the boy said. "Sun tour guide too."

"There's an old fort?" Richard was interested; he liked old ruins of bygone days.

"Yes, master. From British times. Granite ramparts it has and cannons at pirate ships to fire, and pepper pot towers for sentries."

"I'd like to see that," said Richard.

"Day after tomorrow Sun take you can. Car with driver have. Madam Jane also?"

"Oh, no thanks," said Jane. "I'm not interested in historical ruins. I'll swim in the hotel's pool." She turned to Richard. "It's all right. You go with Sun."

He nodded thoughtfully, looked up at Sun whose dark eyes were fixed on him, not on Jane. "Yes, I think I will," he said.

Sun winked. "Early start. Seven o'clock. Long way is."

The next day, at breakfast, Sun came over to their table and, without actually looking at Jane, addressed Richard. "Master, madam, village market today has. Nice to see."

"Ah," said Richard, with a smile. "You want to take us, don't you? Get commission on what we buy?"

"Sorry, master. Cannot. Today busy. Short walk, by yourself together go."

"Yes," said Richard, reaching for Jane's arm. "I think we will, together go."

Sun laughed happily at Richard's response and walked away to talk to a couple at another table.

Jane couldn't remember the last time she'd felt so happy and contented. And the change in Richard was wonderful to see. He seemed far more relaxed and carefree.

They walked around the crowded market holding hands like

a honeymoon couple, ignoring the beckoning stall holders, and marvelling at the psychedelic colours of the swathes of material on display at one stall. Jane treated herself to a wonderful raffia shoulder bag, and Richard bought them both moccasins. The air was filled with the scent of spice and oranges, and the sound of mingled shouts from the street vendors.

They sat outside a pavement café, and drank cups of bitter coffee and indulged in high calorific cakes. Then they each had two glasses of the local brandy, which made them feel heavy and sleepy. Returning to the hotel after the long walk they made love, and then slept in exhausted oblivion.

Waking a few hours later, Richard gently shook his wife. She opened her eyes, groaned, and closed them again. "Come on, you lazy lump," he whispered in her ear, nibbling the lobe.

"Feel sick," she muttered, "too much cake."

"Too much cheap brandy." He laughed.

Jane sat up and was alarmed to feel the room spinning round. Frantically she rushed, just in time, to the bathroom.

"I take it you won't be dining tonight?" Richard called through the door.

"Go away," she whimpered. "Just don't talk about food. I couldn't eat a thing, not ever!"

He laughed again. "Well," he said, "I'm absolutely starving, so I shall go down. I'll ask someone to bring you up a bottle of fruit juice and some aspirin."

She sat up from her kneeling position on the floor in front of the toilet. "But it might be Sun who brings it," she cried. "Oh heavens, he can't see me like this."

Richard's face hardened. He turned on his heel and walked away. Slamming the door of the room, he made his way to the lift and down to the restaurant.

It was a maid who brought the juice and painkillers to the room. She didn't speak English and 'tut-tutted' at Jane, giving her a look of disgust.

#

Jane looked at her watch. She had been asleep for four hours. Although fragile, she felt decidedly improved. *Where on earth is Richard?* she thought. *Dinner must have ended ages ago. Perhaps he's in the bar. Perhaps he has met up with some people and made new friends.* She sighed.

"Such a shame a perfect day has ended this way."

She decided she needed to show a brave face. She showered and changed into a pair of white jeans and floral top. She took the lift down to the ground floor, where the restaurant and bar were located. Feeling rather vulnerable, she glanced around the room, but Richard was nowhere to be seen.

Oh my god, she thought. *I hope he hasn't gone on a bar crawl with some newly-found mate!*

As she walked back to the lift, a blast of heavy rock music halted her and Sun emerged from the disco. He saw her and quickly shut the disco door, cutting off the music. He walked over to her, smiled in a knowing way, and pressed the button to call the lift. "Fourth floor?"

"You know my room number?" she said in surprise.

"Of course. Sun everything knows."

"Well, have you seen my husband?" she asked, wondering why she was trembling as he moved closer. He smelt warm and comforting, a scent of cinnamon.

"In the disco. Drunk, he is. Sun your room come. Now."

It was a statement, not a question.

She shivered, looking at him in a new light. She raised her hand to her face and put her thumb to her lips, uncertain. Sun grinned. The lift arrived and she entered it, followed by Sun, who calmly pressed her floor number and looked deep into her eyes as the door closed.

#

She lay awake, staring at the darkness of the room. *It must be after midnight*, she thought. *What should I tell Richard?*

At last, she heard the key turn in the door, and her husband staggered in. He was drunk, humming a tune to himself. She decided it would be best to feign sleep, as he kicked off his shoes and clambered, fully clothed, into the massive bed, ignoring her.

#

The pinging of the alarm on his smart phone, which Sun had set for him as Richard left the disco, woke him. He shook his head, glanced across at Jane who seemed to be asleep, and got out of bed, surprised to see he was fully dressed.

Well, he thought, looking at his crumpled jeans, *that will save time*. He tore off his shirt, splashed cold water on his face, rummaged in the wardrobe to find a clean T-shirt, put on his shoes, and felt almost ready to face the day. He decided not to wake Jane, closed the door quietly and took the lift downstairs.

Sun was waiting for him. "Good morning, master. Welcome to another day in paradise."

"I told you last night in the disco," Richard said with what sounded like a growl. "Don't call me 'master'. I'm Richard."

"Yes, mast... er... Richard." said Sun. "Glad last night you remember…?"

"Why shouldn't I?" said Richard. "It was fun."

"Thank you," the boy replied with a laugh. "This way come. Car waiting is."

Richard got into the back seat of the car and gingerly leaned against the headrest. "Wake me when we get there," he said, closing his eyes.

Of course, he remembered last night. It had been one of the happiest nights of his life. Sun had sat beside him for a while in the small, darkened disco, the boy's thigh pressing against his in a kind of shared intimacy. Richard had ordered a bottle of the local brandy and happily let Sun fill his glass whenever it was empty. He remembered Sun pulling him on to the floor to dance, something he had not done, even with Jane, for years. He followed Sun's moves, shaking his arms and legs to the music.

Sun had helped him back to the room when the disco closed, patting him on the shoulder and saying, "You're a good man, Richard. I like you," as he unlocked the door and stumbled into the room.

Richard felt a hand on his knee, shaking him. Sun was smiling and leaning over from the front seat of the car. "Wake up," he said. "Arrived we have."

He followed Sun out of the car to a café where a large cup of the island's strong, dark, home grown coffee revived him. "Gosh, Sun," he said admiring the boy's fresh, bright appearance. "How do you do it?"

"Sun always shines, no?" the boy said with a grin. "Around the fort come. You I'll show."

In spite of his hangover, Richard enjoyed the morning. Sun helped him scramble over ruins and they walked together along the broad grassy trail at the top of the fort's ramparts, with its view of the sea dashing against the granite blocks which formed the rampart's sides. He inspected the old cannons, peeped in the pepper pot towers and was fascinated to be walking in history. Time passed quickly, and he was ready when Sun suggested lunch at a small guest house he said was owned by a friend.

They had two beers each and shared a huge baked fish and salad. At the end of the meal, Richard began to feel sleepy. "It's the sun," he said, "very hot!"

"Yes." Sun laughed, as though Richard had made a joke. "A rest you want? Siesta?"

"Yes." He yawned. "But where?"

"Here. A room there is." Sun opened one of the doors at the back of the small restaurant, and beckoned Richard to enter. "No issues," he said, following Richard into the room and shutting the door. "Stay here often I do."

There was only one bed. Richard sat on it gratefully. He kicked off his shoes and stretched out. Sun sat on the bed beside him.

"Sun," said Richard, patting him on his thigh. "You're a good lad."

Sun smiled, touched Richard on his chest and leaned over him.

Richard put his hands up to his shoulders, and tugged him down on top of him.

Later, as they lay naked together side by side on the bed, Richard looked Sun in his eyes and asked, "How did you know?"

"Sun everything knows."

"But how? Did I give a sign? I only just found out myself a few weeks ago. I've been married eight years but this year, with Jane becoming so dowdy and boring, I started looking at the lads in the office. Good looking boys too. I fancied some of them. I didn't know how to tell Jane what was happening to me." He chuckled wryly. "I didn't know how to tell myself."

"But now you do," said Sun. "It's all right."

"To tell her, you mean?"

"Why not?"

"I've got children, twins."

Sun sat up and shrugged his shoulders. "For me one hundred dollars, you have?"

Richard's mood of blissful contentment suddenly vanished and he felt crushed. "What for? You did this for money?"

"Oh no," said Sun with a laugh, his dark eyes twinkling. "Not for that. A reward."

"A reward? What for?"

Sun nudged Richard with his body, making him lie back on the bed and, leaning down put his mouth close to his ear and whispered. "A reward because I didn't sex have with your wife last night when I took her back to your room when you were drunk in the disco. She you loves, Richard. Tell her. Go back to her and tell her who you are."

Richard sighed, nodded, and reached out of the bed for his jeans. He took out his wallet from the back pocket, fumbled to extract a hundred-dollar bill, and pressed it in Sun's hand.

"Thank you," he said. "Whenever I see the sun at home in England, I'll think of you and remember 'Sun everything knows'."

The End

*(**Beach Shorts** by Ruth Smith & Royston Ellis)*